The Cat's Tale

A Jessie Harper Paranormal Cozy Mystery

KJ Cornwall

Hendry Publishing

Contents

2. Chapter One   2
The Librarian's New Page

3. Chapter Two   15
Whispers of the Extraordinary

4. Chapter Three   29
The Cat Speaks

5. Chapter Four   43
Adapting to the Impossible

6. Chapter Five   57
Shadows of the Past

7. Chapter Six   70
The Awakening

8. Chapter Seven   86
The Veil Mended

9. Chapter Eight   101
Guardians of the Veil

10. Epilogue   117

Author's Note

As all the other books in the Jessie Harper Paranormal Cozy Mystery series, it is set in 1930s England. This story's timeline is just after the conclusion of the investigation in *Khan's Clerkenwell Catnapping Caper (Book Four)*. <u>It is therefore suggested you leave reading this novella until after you have read Book Four which will be/was published on December 31, 2024, to avoid reading any spoilers.</u>

At the time of writing, the following books are available in the series:

Murder on the Ferry (Prequel)
Murder at the Vicarage (Book One)
Khan's Christmas Capers (Book Two)
Murder at the Mansion (Book Three)
Khan's Clerkenwell Catnapping Caper (Book Four)
The Vanishing Lady (Book Five)
One further book in this series (Book Six), A Ship Full of Secrets is now on preorder. A further cosy mystery series, the Middleclere Mysteries, set in 1960s England is also now released.

See the updated catalogue at Books2Read.

Chapter One

THE LIBRARIAN'S NEW PAGE

JESSIE HARPER STEPPED INTO the Dale Street Private Investigations Agency office, raindrops still clinging to her like pesky shadows. With a flick of the wrist, she closed her umbrella and gave it a good shake, sending tiny droplets scattering across the doormat. She hung her coat on the rack by the door, its damp fabric making a satisfying swish as it settled against its wooden companions.

"Right on time," she murmured to herself, glancing at the clock whose hands pointed dutifully to the start of another investigative day. Jessie moved towards her desk with the quiet confidence of someone who had found her true calling outside the hushed corridors of a library.

Her desk greeted her with the familiarity of an old friend, albeit one that always seemed to need something from her. She sat down, easing into the chair that had moulded itself to her form through many hours of diligent sleuthing. Her hazel eyes surveyed the stack of case files before her, each folder a story begging to be read, understood, and resolved.

With slender fingers, Jessie sifted through the pile, the edges of the folders frayed from frequent handling. They whispered under her touch, a papery susurrus that was as comforting as it was constant. She paused when she came across a note, pinned to the front of a particularly thick file. The paper was creased from being opened and re-folded multiple times, evidence of a recent client's anxious rereading.

Her brow knit together in a thoughtful frown, Jessie leaned in closer, the words on the page pulling her deep into their narrative. It wasn't just the spidery handwriting that captivated her; it was the mystery wrapped within, a puzzle only she could piece together. "Hmm..." she hummed, a habit picked up from her days among the bookshelves, where every problem seemed to warrant a vocal pondering.

"Curiouser and curiouser," Jessie quipped to the empty room, a line borrowed from a favourite fictional character and repurposed for her own investigative adventures. Her voice was soft but carried a wry edge, a hallmark of her wit that often surfaced even in solitude.

The note detailed an encounter most peculiar   a phantom melody heard in an old music hall long after the last note should have faded. Jessie tapped the note with her finger, her mind already turning over the possibilities. Could it be a trick of acoustics, or perhaps something more spectral?

"Looks like it's not just books that hold secrets," Jessie said, tucking a stray strand of auburn hair behind her ear. As she placed the note back on top of the file, she smiled faintly, ready to unravel yet another enigma in a world where the past was never truly silent.

The rain's gentle tapping against the pane brought a rhythmic peace to the office. Jessie Harper, seated at her desk, found her thoughts wandering amidst the steady cadence. The pitter-patter of droplets mingled with memories, taking her back to the quiet hush of Liverpool's library aisles—the place where she once spent her days surrounded by the comforting scent of old books, their musty perfume a reminder of countless stories and secrets.

"Another lifetime," she murmured with a wistful smile, her gaze lingering on the rain-streaked window, as if it were a portal to her past. Her thoughts then turned to the last investigation: the catnapping caper in Clerkenwell, London, when Khan had been invaluable, as always, but this time he went beyond the call of duty in an undercover role infiltrating London's feline community.

Jessie's colleagues in the detective agency had taken a few days off whilst she decided to reorganise the office files. *Lucky George, lucky Isabel and her sister Agnes, the new receptionist. Detective Sergeant Bill Roberts too*, she thought as she mentally ticked off the agencies' detectives, receptionist and her mentor Bill Roberts of the Liverpool City Police. *My, how the agency had grown from the start when it was only me and George with some help from Bill*, she thought.

Khan, the enigmatic feline perched on the windowsill, chose that moment to stretch. His black fur gleamed, and he extended one paw after the other with a luxuriousness that only cats possess. He yawned widely, and for a brief second, his sharp teeth caught the grey light filtering through the clouds outside, giving him an almost otherworldly appearance.

"Quite the display, Khan," Jessie commented, her voice tinged with amusement. "Are you trying to remind me that there's more to life than old files and rainy days?"

Khan's green eyes fixed on Jessie, and for a fleeting moment, it was as if he understood every nuance of her words.

This wasn't new for Jessie as for some time Khan had talked first with Jessie, then George – otherwise known as GJ, followed by Bill, and more recently, Isabel.

However, the knowing glint in his stare seemed to penetrate beyond the surface, hinting at an ancient wisdom hidden beneath his sleek exterior. Then, just as quickly as the moment had come, it passed, and he settled back into his favourite spot, his tail flicking idly, dismissing the world around him. *What an enigma!* Jessie thought.

"Or perhaps you're simply pondering your next meal," Jessie said, chuckling at the thought of her cat's likely less-mystical motivations. But even as she bantered with the silent Khan, her heart warmed at the sight of him—a constant companion in her sometimes-lonely quest for answers among the shadows of the paranormal.

Jessie rose from her chair, the creak of the aged leather a familiar sound in the quiet room. She crossed to the kitchenette tucked away in the corner of the office—a nook that had become her sanctuary when the puzzles of the paranormal world grew too dense. As she filled the kettle and set it on the stove, her movements were methodical, comforting in their predictability.

She scooped the tea leaves from the caddy, the scent of Ceylon rising to greet her as she dropped them into the teapot—a fragrance that never failed to transport her back to the musty, book-lined shelves of the reference library where she once worked. With the kettle's gentle whistle, Jessie poured the scalding water over the tea leaves, watching as the steam danced upwards, mingling with the humid air.

Humming a tune that was half-remembered, half-improvised, Jessie waited patiently for the tea to mash. Pouring the golden liquid into her favourite porcelain cup, she then stirred honey into the brew, the spoon chiming against the cup like a tiny bell in a distant cathedral. The simple act of making tea was an anchor in her often-whimsical life, a moment of peace amid the storm of spectral secrets and whispers of the unknown.

Cradling the warm cup in her hands, she returned to her desk where papers lay scattered like leaves in autumn. Khan watched her from his perch, his eyes half-closed but ever observant. Jessie sipped the tea, feeling the warmth spread through her fingers and radiate up her arms, a balm against the cool draught that played about the edges of the old office.

"Nothing like a good cuppa to make everything right with the world, eh?" Jessie said, addressing the cat as though he were an old friend privy to the inner workings of her mind—which, in a way, he was.

Settling back into her work, Jessie picked up her pen, its nib poised above a fresh notepad. She jotted down notes with care, her handwriting a mix of librarian's precision and sleuth's shorthand. Each word was a step closer to unlocking the mysteries that awaited her savvy and intuition.

The tea continued to exude its heat, a small beacon of comfort as the shadows lengthened and the rain's rhythm persisted outside. Jessie smiled, feeling centred amidst the chaos of clues and conjectures, her spirit steadied by the simple pleasures of the afternoon ritual.

With the steam from her tea rising in gentle swirls, Jessie leaned over the clutter of case files that covered her desk. She was so absorbed in the details of her notes that she didn't notice Khan's silent contemplation from his cosy windowsill vantage point. Without warning, he stirred from his feline reverie, stretching out with a fluid grace that only cats possess.

In one smooth motion, Khan leapt from the sill, landing on the desk with a soft thud that barely disturbed the papers beneath his paws. He sauntered toward a manila folder that lay slightly askew from the rest and gave it a deliberate nudge, pushing it towards Jessie with an air of authority.

"Ah, what is it now, Mr Mysterious?" Jessie chuckled warmly, her gaze shifting from the file to the sleek black cat who now sat with a regal tilt to his head. She reached out and scratched behind his ears, eliciting a contented purr that vibrated through the quiet room.

"You're always full of advice, aren't you?" she mused aloud, her voice tinged with affection as she glanced at the file Khan had singled out. Her fingers traced the edges of the paper, feeling the slight wear of frequent handling. "Let's see what wisdom you've got for me today."

Khan responded with a knowing look, his tail curling around his body like a velvet rope, the tip tapping gently against the wooden surface of the desk. It was moments like these—when the veil between the ordinary and the extraordinary seemed to thin—that Jessie felt a deep connection to the enigmatic feline by her side.

The shrill ring of the telephone cleaved through the tranquillity of the Dale Street Private Investigations Agency office. Jessie Harper, with the ease of a seasoned professional, set aside the notes she had been scribbling and reached for the receiver. "Dale Street Private Investigations, Jessie speaking," she answered, her voice as crisp as the pages of the well-loved mystery novels she once tended.

"Miss Harper, thank goodness... I didn't know who else to call." The voice on the other end trembled like leaves in a storm, words tumbling out in a frantic cascade. Jessie's hand moved deftly, her pen gliding over the notepad as she collected the details: strange occurrences, voices in the night, and a shadow that seemed to have a will of its own.

"Understood," Jessie reassured the caller, her tone a blend of empathy and professionalism. "Where do you live?"

"The Isle of Skye. I read about your agency in the newspaper."

"Oh, my goodness that's a long way from Liverpool. We are a bit short-staffed at the moment, is it alright if we try to get to you next week?"

"That's fine. I'm Mrs McTavish by the way, Fiona McTavish," the caller said.

"Thank you, Mrs McTavish let me make a note of your telephone number so we can inform you of our arrival next week," Jessie said.

She replaced the receiver, the echo of the dial tone still hanging in the air. Leaning back in her chair, Jessie let out a slow breath, her thoughts coalescing around the peculiarities of the new case. Khan, still the silent confidant, remained perched on the corner of the desk, his green eyes fixed on his human companion. His tail, an elegant barometer of his mood, twitched ever so slightly, as if tapping out a secret code only he understood.

"Seems we've got a whispering shadow on our hands, Khan," Jessie mused, her gaze drifting to the rain-streaked window. She could almost see the tendrils of mystery curling in with the fog.

Khan blinked slowly, regarding Jessie with what might be considered a feline semblance of thoughtfulness. Although he offered no verbal response... yet... there was a sense of solidarity in his silent vigil; an acknowledgment that, whatever this new enigma entailed, they would unravel it together.

Jessie knew Khan would speak to her only when he deemed it necessary but that was no barrier to Jessie speaking with Khan. "Alright then," Jessie said, standing up with renewed determination. "Let's get to the bottom of this." Her smile was small but determined—the kind of smile that had seen her through many a spectral puzzle—and with Khan by her side, she felt ready to face the unseen once more.

Jessie's fingers danced over the manila folders with the gentle grace of an expert librarian, her eyes scanning each label before tucking them away into the filing cabinet. The cases varied from the peculiar to the downright otherworldly, but all were in a day's work for Jessie Harper. She plucked a bulky file—'The Case of the Weeping Walls'—from the stack and set it aside; that one merited further scrutiny.

"More secrets than a locked diary, this one," she murmured, running a hand through her hair. A soft chuckle escaped her lips as she imagined the walls spilling their tales like old gossips at a book club.

Outside, the rain had intensified into an assertive downpour, its steady drumming against the glass a comforting counterpoint to the silence of the office. The rain stopped as a thickening fog crept along Dale Street, wrapping the outside world in a blanket of swirling grey. Inside, the light waned, causing shadows to stretch and play across the room's corners.

"Looks like we're in for a real peasouper," Jessie noted, squinting against the dimness. She stood up, stretching her legs, and flipped the switch on the brass desk lamp. Its golden glow cast a warm circle of light, pushing back against the encroaching gloom.

Khan, meanwhile, had decided that enough was enough with regards to the height of his perch. With a fluid motion that belied his regal demeanour, he hopped down from the desk. His black fur absorbed the lamplight, giving him an ethereal quality as he slipped silently across the floor, heading straight for the cast iron radiator.

"Ah, to have your priorities straight," Jessie said, admiring Khan's single-minded pursuit of warmth. She watched with a smile as he settled into one of his favourite spots, the heat causing his sleek fur to shimmer slightly. He curled up, the tip of his tail neatly wrapping around his front paws—a picture of feline contentment.

"Comfortable, are we?" Jessie teased, her voice laced with affection. Khan merely blinked back at her, his eyes half-closed in bliss. There was something about the cat's steady presence that never failed to ease the chill from her bones, much like the tea she sipped throughout the day.

"Alright, you've got the right idea," Jessie conceded, turning back to her desk to jot down a final note. "A good sleuth knows when to pause and recharge, even if it's just to keep the cold at bay."

The ticking clock on the wall signalled the march of time, but within the cosy confines of the office, with Khan by the radiator and the fog pressing against the windows, Jessie felt a tranquil detachment from the hustle of the world outside. And in that moment, she knew there was nowhere else she'd rather be. She was content with her own company... and Khan's of course. She also knew George Jenkins would understand as her business partner, fellow sleuth, and (say it quietly) romantic interest.

Jessie's gaze lingered on the clock's hands, inching toward closure on another day's mysteries. With a contented sigh that echoed slightly in the quiet room, she stood up and began the familiar ritual of tidying her desk. Each case file was tapped into a neat stack, the papers whispering secrets as they slid together. She clicked her pen closed with a decisive snap, the sound a period at the end of an industrious sentence.

"Time to feed the stomach as well as the mind," Jessie murmured to herself, her voice carrying the melody of a job well done. She moved towards the kitchenette, her movements unhurried, basking in the satisfaction of order restored.

Pausing by the door, she couldn't help but glance back at the office. The shelves lined with paranormal paraphernalia, the walls adorned with maps marked with ley lines and mystical hotspots – it had become more than just a workspace; it was a sanctuary. Since George and she had settled into their new arrangement, with separate bedrooms allowing each their peculiar habits and schedules, the office had transformed into a shared niche of collaboration and camaraderie.

In the kitchenette, pots clinked gently against one another, a culinary symphony performed for an audience of one. Jessie hummed under her breath, a tune without words, as she set about creating a simple but nourishing meal for herself. The sizzle of onions hitting the pan filled the air with homely aromas, the scents weaving around her like comforting arms.

She peered through the window into the foggy Liverpool evening, the streetlights casting halos in the mist. It was a scene from a Charles Dickens novel, one where the city whispered its secrets to those patient enough to listen. And Jessie, with her librarian's heart and sleuth's soul, felt an unshakeable connection to the highways, the byways and the hidden alleys that threaded through the historic seaport.

"Looks like pea soup out there," Jessie commented, half expecting Khan to toss a witty retort about dinner choices. But the cat merely padded silently to the windowsill, his black fur blending with the shadows as he settled down, a silent sentinel by her side.

Jessie smiled, knowing that Khan's company was as much a part of her routine as the tea leaves were to the pot. As she stirred a fresh pot, the spoon clinking softly against the sides, she knew that whatever the fog might conceal, together they would uncover it. Khan's tail flicked once, a sign she interpreted as agreement, or perhaps just the twitch of a dream about chasing spectral mice.

"Ready for a break, Khan?" Jessie asked, though the answer seemed evident in his relaxed posture. He shifted slightly, the green of his eyes catching the light as if to affirm their partnership in all things, mundane and mysterious.

With supper simmering on the stove, Jessie allowed herself a moment of quiet reflection. Here, in this cosy room with the aroma of cooking in the air and the comfort of her enigmatic feline friend, she was home. Home to think, to dream, and to solve the unsolvable. Liverpool's fog might obscure the city from sight, but for Jessie Harper, it only added another layer of intrigue to unravel.

After dinner, the night awaited, ready to unfold its mysteries before them. Khan would be right there, his presence a constant in the ever-shifting world of the paranormal investigator.

The enticing scent of lean strips of fillets of beef cooked in wine and onions wafted through the small kitchenette as Jessie plated two generous servings, the steam curling up like the fog outside. She carried the plates into the dining area before scraping one of the meals into Khan's bowl. "I know you like that, Khan, but don't tell George because it's his favourite too."

They settled at the table, the clink of cutlery and the soft murmur of their conversation a familiar duet. Khan, ever the observant sentinel, remained perched on the windowsill, his silhouette outlined by the streetlamps filtering through the fog.

"So," Jessie began, sipping her water, "that last case—the one with the kidnapped cats in London—turned out quite the adventure, didn't it?"

Khan chuckled, "Adventure? You could say that. It was different, for sure."

"Exactly that," Jessie said, her eyes sparkling with mirth as she remembered the incredulous look on George's face when he first found out it was a corrupt London detective who was the mastermind behind the whole caper.

"True," Khan conceded, shaking his head in bemusement. "I'll never understand why things like that don't surprise you but I suppose that's why you're the expert in the paranormal and I'm just the brains in the organisation."

"Brains with a soft spot for George, might I add." Jessie teased him gently, a witty edge to her friendly ribbing.

"Let's not spread that around, shall we?" Khan said with mock sternness, though the twinkle in his eye betrayed his fondness for their absent friend.

Jessie laughed, the sound mingling with the patter of rain against the windowpane—a soothing backdrop to their mealtime banter. As they continued to discuss the peculiarities of their recent case, the night deepened around them, wrapping the Dale Street Private Investigations Agency in a cocoon of warmth and camaraderie, the mysteries of the day giving way to the contentment of the evening.

Chapter Two

WHISPERS OF THE EXTRAORDINARY

JESSIE HARPER WAS NESTLED among a fortress of cardboard and manila, her desk at Dale Street Private Investigations Agency strewn with the detritus of mysteries long since solved. As she methodically worked her way through the stack of old case files—each one a story, a puzzle pieced together—her fingers stumbled upon an anomaly. A particularly dusty folder lay buried beneath a mountain of routine investigations, its edges worn and softened with time. The label, though faded, struck a chord in Jessie's ever-curious mind: "Unexplained Phenomena."

She hesitated for the barest of moments, as if the folder itself was a Pandora's box of forgotten lore. But curiosity, as it often did with Jessie, won out over caution. She carefully lifted the cover, a small cloud of dust motes swirling up to dance in the slanting light that filtered through the blinds.

"Hello, what's this then?" she murmured to herself as she eyed the contents with growing interest. Each report was more intriguing than the last: accounts of ghostly sightings that sent shivers down her spine, sketches of mysterious symbols that seemed to whisper of ancient secrets. Jessie leaned closer, her auburn hair spilling over her shoulders as she rifled through the papers, the musty scent of aged ink and paper filling her senses.

"Spooky," she muttered with a wry smile, her sense of whimsy always close at hand despite the eerie subject matter. It was like stepping into a world where the lines between reality and the paranormal blurred into obscurity.

Her excitement grew stronger, a charge in the air that even the office's familiar surroundings couldn't contain. Jessie grabbed a notepad from the jumble on her desk and began jotting down notes with fervour, her handwriting looping across the page in quick, thoughtful strokes. Figures and facts, dates and witness statements—all were grist for the mill of her insatiable intellect.

"Could be something to this," Jessie pondered aloud. "Or could just be a load of old cobblers." Yet she couldn't deny the pull of possibility, the allure of the unknown that had led her from the quiet order of library shelves to the thrilling chaos of private investigation.

With each piece of evidence she unearthed, the gears in her mind turned faster, racing toward connections unseen but deeply felt. In every shadowed corner of Liverpool, it seemed, lurked stories waiting to be told, phantoms eager to reveal their truths to those willing to listen. Jessie Harper, with her penchant for both knowledge and the inexplicable, was all too ready to oblige.

Jessie pushed back her chair, the legs scraping gently against the office's old wooden floor. She stood and stretched languidly, arms reaching towards the ceiling as if to gather the energy that hung there, vibrant with dusty motes of sunlight. A yawn escaped her, more from contentment than fatigue—her mind was too alight with curiosity for tiredness to take hold.

Turning toward the window, Jessie watched the fog outside. It embraced Liverpool like an old friend, wrapping its ethereal arms around the city's architecture in a ghostly hug. Nudging the window open with her elbow, she let the cool breath of the outside world fill her lungs. The air smelled of rain-soaked cobblestones, the close-by Mersey, and whispered secrets.

"Time for a little fieldwork," she murmured to herself, thinking of 'The Magic Box'. The bookshop had always been a trove of esoteric knowledge—a perfect complement to her librarian's love for the order within chaos. With a decisive nod, she grabbed her trusty notepad and pen, tucking them into her coat pocket.

Buttoning up her coat against the chill, Jessie left the office, her boots clicking a steady rhythm on the hardwood floors then down the stairs before meeting the muted resistance of the fog-dampened streets. The mist curled playfully around her ankles, as though guiding her steps through the labyrinth of Liverpool's alleys and thoroughfares.

She pulled her coat tighter, the fabric enveloping her slender frame. Jessie's hazel eyes sparkled with anticipation as she navigated the familiar yet ever-mysterious path to the bookshop. Each echo of her footsteps on the granite paving slabs seemed to be in conversation with the shrouded city, exchanging tales of times gone by.

"Best not dawdle," she chided herself with a wry smile, quickening her pace. The thought of what arcane wisdom might lay waiting within the bookshop's musty depths spurred her onward. Her breath formed tiny clouds that mingled with the fog, each exhalation a fleeting ghost to accompany her journey.

"Bit nippy today, isn't it?" Jessie observed, though no one was around to agree or disagree. She often found solace in giving voice to her thoughts; it made her feel less alone when Khan, her sole confidant and feline overseer, wasn't perched nearby, offering silent counsel with his emerald gaze.

Her anticipation built as the outline of 'The Magic Box' began to materialise out of the mist, its windows aglow with the promise of hidden knowledge. Jessie's heart picked up its tempo, beating a dance of discovery as she reached for the door handle, ready to plunge once more into the enigmatic embrace of the unknown.

The bell above the door chimed a soft, welcoming note as Jessie Harper stepped over the threshold into bookshop. The scent of old paper and smouldering incense wrapped around her like a well-loved shawl, infusing her senses with a cocktail of nostalgia and mystery. Her eyes adjusted to the dim light, and she inhaled deeply, savouring the unique aroma that only a trove of ancient literature could produce.

"Back again, Jessie?" The shopkeeper's voice was as textured as the leather bindings that lined the shelves, with an underlying note of amusement at her predictability.

"Can't stay away from the allure of the unknown," Jessie replied, her tone laced with the familiar warmth of their ongoing rapport. She offered him a knowing smile before turning towards her destination—the section on Egyptian mythology and supernatural phenomena.

"Anything in particular today?" the shopkeeper called after her, polishing a pair of spectacles with his handkerchief.

"More pieces for the puzzle," Jessie said over her shoulder, her wit sharpening the edges of her words as she vanished into the maze of towering bookcases.

Within the hallowed alcoves, Jessie's fingers danced across the bindings, her touch as reverent as a pianist upon the keys. She traced the embossed titles, feeling the impressions like ancient braille speaking secrets directly to her soul. With each volume she considered, a surge of exhilaration pulsed through her. Here, amid the stories of bygone eras, Jessie felt the rush of being on the cusp of revelation of something she did not yet know.

"Ah, what do we have here?" Jessie murmured, extracting a weighty tome bound in cracked leather. The gold lettering had faded, but the thrill of discovery ignited within her, bright and beckoning. She added it to the crook of her arm, where two other promising candidates already nestled snugly.

"Bit of light reading, then?" Jessie quipped under her breath, though Khan wasn't there to offer his silent, feline snarkiness. She imagined his green eyes following her every move, discerning and wise, as if urging her to delve deeper, to look beyond the veil of the mundane.

Her collection grew, an eclectic mix of dusty lore and arcane symbolism—a testament to Jessie's relentless curiosity and her dedication to uncovering the truth that lurked in the shadows of the ordinary. Each selection was a potential key, a thread that might lead her through the intricate tapestry of the paranormal enigma she was so eager to unravel.

"Looks like you've got your hands full," the shopkeeper noted as Jessie approached the counter, her arms cradling the precious cargo of knowledge.

"Let's hope they're as enlightening as they are hefty," Jessie said, flashing a grin that spoke of adventures yet to come and mysteries waiting to be solved. With her new acquisitions tucked under her arm, she was ready to dive headfirst into the cryptic depths that beckoned her forward.

BACK AT THE DALE Street Private Investigations Agency, Jessie Harper dropped her trove of newly acquired knowledge onto the desk with a satisfying thud. She settled into her chair with the kind of reverence usually reserved for sacred ceremonies, her fingertips gingerly caressing the cracked leather spines as she lined the books up like soldiers ready for inspection. With a soft exhale, Jessie flipped open the topmost volume, its pages promising secrets as they turned.

"Right," she said, her eyes bursting with scholarly fervour. "Let's see what you're hiding."

The world around her faded into a blur as she became immersed in tales spun from a time when gods walked among mortals and magic was as common as the air breathed by those ancient peoples. Symbols that had danced on the edges of her understanding now began to take on clear shapes and meanings. Jessie broke her cardinal rule by scribbling notes in the margins—hieroglyphs, pentagrams, and otherworldly sigils—each one a breadcrumb on the path to unravelling the unexplained phenomena that had piqued her curiosity.

From his perch on the windowsill, Khan observed Jessie with a quiet intensity only a creature of his mystical heritage could muster. The late afternoon sun filtered through the mist outside, casting his sleek black fur in a halo of light that seemed almost eerie. His tail flicked, betraying his thoughts as he watched the woman who had become both charge and companion.

"Careful, Jessie," Khan's eyes seemed to say, his gaze unwavering. "Some truths can't be unread."

Jessie, lost in her studious concentration, was oblivious to the silent conversation. Instead, she traced a finger down a page describing an invocation so potent it was said to summon spirits from the Duat itself. Her breath caught in her throat; this was the kind of information that stoked the fires of her passion for the paranormal—a passion that had driven her from a life organising bookshelves to one filled with the pursuit of the extraordinary.

"Jessie," Khan finally said in a voice that seemed different. It was laced with both pride and a hint of caution. It was a tone that spoke of lived centuries, of wisdom gathered like precious jewels. "Remember, knowledge is as much a key as it is a lock."

"Of course, Khan," she replied, not looking up from the text but smiling in acknowledgment of his concern. "But we can't deny the allure of unlocking doors long closed, can we?"

"Indeed, we cannot," he conceded, his green eyes narrowing slightly as if to accentuate his point. His presence on the windowsill, though silent as the fog that was again clinging to Liverpool's streets, was a steadfast reminder of the balance between curiosity and heedfulness—a balance Jessie knew all too well but often found herself teetering on the edge of.

With that tacit exchange hanging in the air like the scent of incense, Jessie returned to her research, and Khan continued to watch over her, guardian and guide through the veils of reality and beyond.

Time slipped by unnoticed as Jessie Harper delved deeper into the enigmas of the paranormal. Her desk had transformed into a landscape of scattered notes and open books, each page a topography of esoteric knowledge waiting to be charted. She hunched over a particularly worn volume, her hair falling like a curtain around her concentrated face. The only sound in the room was the soft scratch of her pen and the occasional murmur that escaped her lips, a testament to her unwavering quest.

"Could it be?" she whispered, tracing a line of hieroglyphs with a fingertip. "The symbol of Thoth... or merely a scribe's flourish?"

Khan observed from the windowsill, his silhouette cut sharp against the greying light outside. He watched as Jessie pieced together fragments of lore, her eyes reflecting the passion of her quest. She was so engrossed in her studies that the world beyond these four walls might as well have ceased to exist.

"Ah, now this is fascinating," Jessie mused aloud, tapping the page where an illustration of an eye—similar to the one watching her—seemed to stare back. It was the Eye of Horus, a symbol of protection, royal power, and good health. Yet, as Jessie knew all too well, symbols often held more than one meaning.

As if on cue, a dull ache began to throb at her temples. With a soft sigh, Jessie leaned back in her chair and closed her eyes for a moment, her fingers massaging her forehead in small circles. She then glanced up at Khan, whose enigmatic expression seemed to soften just for her.

"Quite the mystery we have here, isn't it?" she said, a wry smile playing on her lips.

Khan tilted his head, the corners of his green eyes crinkling in what could only be described as feline amusement. His tail gave a solitary, deliberate twitch, as if to say, "Indeed, but you wouldn't want it any other way."

"Your wisdom, as always, is impeccable," Jessie chuckled, appreciating the silent dialogue they shared. Then she hesitated. *Is it silence or telepathy at work?* Khan's presence alone was comforting —a grounding force amid the whirlwind of arcane secrets swirling around them.

"Though I do sometimes wonder," she continued, giving Khan a conspiratorial glance, "if you're not the one behind half these mysteries, just to keep things interesting."

Khan's purring response seemed to convey both a snarky retort and an affirmation of their bond. Jessie couldn't help but laugh softly, knowing full well that the enigmatic feline adored her just as much as she did him. It was this unspoken understanding that fuelled her determination to untangle the web of the paranormal—with Khan as her steadfast companion.

The shadows lengthened over the office walls of the detective agency, creeping along the bookshelves and pooling in the corners like curious spectres. With the day's light ebbing away, Jessie reached for the small brass lamp that sat on her cluttered desk and clicked it to life. A soft, golden hue spilled across the room, bathing the chaotic jumble of case files, notes, and ancient lore in a cosy glow. The atmosphere, now intimate and inviting, hummed with a quiet energy—a prelude to secrets soon to be whispered.

She leaned back in her chair, feeling the warmth of the lamp cut through the chill of the evening, and exhaled a slow breath. It was as if the room itself had drawn a protective circle around her, shielding her from the mundane world and ushering her into the realm of the unexplained.

As the silence settled comfortably around her, Khan, the black-furred enigma with eyes that held millennia, decided it was time to break his own stillness. He stretched languidly, his sleek body elongating before curling back into its compact elegance. In one fluid motion that defied the laws of gravity—and perhaps, decorum—he leapt onto the desk, landing with the soft sound of paws against wood.

"Decided to join me up close, have you?" Jessie remarked with an affectionate smile, reaching out instinctively to smooth a hand over Khan's shimmering coat.

Khan, however, was not in the mood for idle strokes or playful banter. He fixed Jessie with a stare so intense it seemed he could see straight through to her core. His green eyes, now mirroring the lamplight, flickered with an ethereal intelligence. It was a look that spoke volumes without a single word uttered—yet.

"Alright then," Jessie nodded, recognising the gravity of the moment. "I'm all ears."

The room seemed to hold its breath, and even the flickering beam from the lamp paused as if in anticipation of the tale about to unravel from the lips of a cat who had walked the sands of time long before Liverpool was a small fishing port and the liver bird myth had never yet been heard of.

Jessie leaned forward, the worn fabric of her chair whispering softly against her pleated skirt. Her heart tapped a quick rhythm against her ribcage, echoing the ticking of the clock on the wall. The anticipation was almost tangible in the air, like the electric charge before a thunderstorm. Excitement mingled with a hint of nervousness as she considered the enigma that was Khan—her feline companion who defied explanation.

"Khan," Jessie started, her voice barely above a whisper, "what is it you're about to tell me?"

With the solemnity of a scholar unearthing ancient secrets, Khan's gaze never wavered from Jessie's eyes. His tail gave a small flick, and then, unexpectedly, he spoke, his voice different once more. This time it possessed a deep timbre that seemed to resonate with the wisdom of ages past.

"Jessie, my dear," he began, his snarky tone taking on a cadence of reverence, "what I am about to reveal stems from a time when the world was young, and magic was as common as the sands of the Nile."

Her breath caught in her throat; she had never heard him speak quite like this before. Each word he spoke painted images in her mind of golden landscapes and towering pyramids, of pharaohs and deities whose names echoed through history.

"Long before your historians penned their first chronicle, Ancient Egypt thrived with powers that your modern world can scarcely imagine," Khan continued, his eyes glowing like emeralds set in the shadows of the room.

"What you call 'paranormal' or 'supernatural' were simply... normal or natural for us."

Jessie found herself entranced, her former life as a librarian providing no anchor in the face of such revelations. The spines of the books around her seemed to lean in closer, as though they too were eager to absorb the story from one who had lived it.

"Tell me everything," she urged, her wit giving way to wide-eyed wonder.

"Patience, Jessie," Khan admonished gently, his whiskers twitching with the semblance of a smile. "All in due time. For now, let us start at the beginning, where gods walked among mortals, and magic was as easy to grasp as the reeds by the river..."

And so, under the warm glow of the lamp and the steadfast tick of the clock, Jessie listened, her world expanding with each ancient word that fell from Khan's lips, each sentence weaving a tapestry richer than any she had ever known.

Khan's tail made a slow, rhythmic sweep across the stack of notes on the desk as he concluded his enthralling narrative. "And that, Jessie, is merely the overture to a symphony of secrets," he said, his tone dipping into the deeper octaves of mystery.

Jessie leaned back in her chair, the creak of the aged wood beneath her acting as a gentle reminder of the reality she momentarily left behind. Her eyes reflected the dance of candlelight around the room, mirroring the flicker of awe and intrigue within.

"More?" she whispered, almost afraid that asking would break the spell Khan had cast with his words.

"Indeed, more," Khan affirmed, his eyes half-closed, as if privy to visions of times yet to unfold. "But not tonight. The night is deep, and even enigmatic felines must respect the rhythms of this world."

Jessie chuckled, her mind still adrift in the sea of ancient lore he had revealed. She rose from her chair, stretching limbs stiffened by hours of rapt attention. "You do realise you've just set my curiosity ablaze," she said, her voice tinged with both exasperation and affection. "How am I supposed to sleep now?"

"Ah, but the sweetest dreams are those laced with the promise of discovery," Khan replied, hopping gracefully off the desk to saunter towards the windowsill. With a graceful leap, he perched on the edge, his silhouette an elegant contrast against the moonlit fog outside.

"Tomorrow, we shall delve deeper," he continued, casting a glance back at Jessie. "For now, rest and let the whispers of the ancients guide your dreams."

Jessie nodded, the weight of her eyelids suddenly reminding her of the late hour. "Thank you, Khan," she said, her voice a soft murmur filled with gratitude. "For everything."

"Think nothing of it," Khan replied, his snarkiness softened by the night's revelations. "After all, what are friends for, if not to unveil the mysteries of the cosmos?"

With a smile playing upon her lips, Jessie extinguished the lamp, plunging the room into a comfortable darkness punctuated only by the soft glow of Liverpool's slumbering streetlights filtering through the fog and the window. She felt the bond between them deepen, a connection that transcended time and logic—a librarian, now amateur sleuth, and a magical talking cat, linked by the allure of the paranormal.

As Jessie retreated to her bedroom, leaving Khan to his nocturnal reveries, the promise of more tales lingered in the air like the scent of ancient papyrus. The next chapter of their journey awaited, brimming with the allure of secrets yet to be told, and Jessie Harper knew that sleep would be a mere interlude in the grand adventure that was unfolding before her.

Chapter Three

THE CAT SPEAKS

THE NEXT DAY, JESSIE Harper sank into the embrace of her office chair, her fingertips caressing the familiar cracked leather. She gazed through the rain-streaked window, watching as tendrils of fog danced a ghostly ballet on the street beyond. Her mind wandered back to the bizarre twists of one of their early cases, which had involved more spectral apparitions than she'd have liked.

"Curiouser and curiouser," she murmured, echoing a favourite saying from her librarian days, where mysteries were set in novels and were mere fiction, not her daily bread.

The rhythmic tapping of paws against wood drew her attention away from the grey veil outside. Khan, the enigmatic feline with whom she shared both home and office space, was approaching. His sleek black fur seemed to absorb the room's weak light, while his emerald eyes shimmered like beacons in the gloom.

With the grace of an acrobat—or perhaps something far older and more mystic—Khan leapt onto Jessie's desk. The impact was slight but enough to make the papers flutter like timid birds caught in a sudden gust of wind.

"Jessie," he intoned, his voice deep and oddly resonant for a creature of his size. It filled the room, seeming to come from everywhere at once, wrapping around her like the fog outside.

She stilled, struck by the intensity of his gaze. It wasn't just the peculiar green of his eyes; it was the knowledge, the ancient wisdom that lurked within them. Here was no ordinary house pet, but a guide through the shadowy realms they had often traversed together.

"Khan?" She leaned in, her wit on standby, prepared for one of his snarky observations. "What cryptic puzzle are we unravelling today?"

"Indeed, Jessie," Khan began, his tone laced with the affectionate condescension only a cat—or perhaps a pharaoh—could muster. "There are things you must hear."

She chuckled softly, her eyes sparking with intrigue. Every time Khan spoke, it was an invitation to peel back another layer of reality, to glimpse the cogs and gears of the paranormal world they so eagerly explored together.

"Then speak, O' wise one," she said, her voice playful yet edged with genuine respect. "I'm all ears."

Khan nodded once, solemnly, as if acknowledging the gravity of what was to come. "In the times of old, when sand swallowed secrets and the Nile whispered tales of eternity..."

Jessie listened, enthralled, as the room around them seemed to fade, giving way to a spectacle only Khan could conjure. The walls of the Dale Street Private Investigations Agency melted into the background, and for a moment, just a fleeting instant, they were not in Liverpool anymore, but somewhere far more ancient and mysterious.

Jessie's eyebrows arched, a silent testament to her as-tonishment as Khan's voice, deep and melodic, took on the cadence of an ancient storyteller. She leaned forward instinctively, her curiosity now a living thing that seemed to perch on the edge of the desk, as tangible as the cat before her. The fog outside was forgotten, the peculiarities of old cases fading into insignificance as she absorbed the gravity of Khan's narrative.

"Picture the pyramids, Jessie," Khan intoned, his emerald gaze never leaving her. "Not as they are now, weathered by time, but newborn, their limestone cladding agleam in the relentless sun."

A hush fell over the room, punctuated only by the distant rattle of trams and the Liverpool Overhead Railway that trickled through the windowpane. In her mind's eye, Jessie saw not just the grandeur of these structures but the pulse of daily existence that thrummed around them. She could almost hear the rhythmic chink of chisel against stone, the murmur of voices rising from the labourers as they toiled.

"Along the banks of the great Nile, life teemed," Khan continued, each word meticulously chosen, vibrant with life. "Merchants hawked their wares, fishermen cast their nets, and lotus flowers bobbed gently on the surface of the water, their fragrance mingling with the scent of fresh bread and roasting fish."

Jessie's senses were alight with the imagery; she could feel the heat of the Egyptian sun on her skin, taste the tang of dust and sweat in the air. Khan's tale wove an enchanting spell, one that transcended the limits of time and space, ensnaring her within its golden threads.

"Such was the world from whence I came," Khan said softly, his tone imbued with a nostalgia that belied his usual snarkiness. "A land where gods walked among mortals, and my kind—far more than mere felines—were revered as conduits to the divine."

Jessie's heartbeat skipped along with a rhythm akin to the flow of the ancient river itself. Each sentence Khan spoke was like the discovery of a hidden chamber, filled with treasures untold. His words were not just descriptors; they were portals, gateways to a past that suddenly felt as real and as immediate as the office in which they sat.

"Remarkable," she whispered, hardly aware she had spoken aloud, her thoughtful demeanour giving way to the sheer awe of the moment. Her pen hovered above her open journal, poised to capture the essence of Khan's revelations, yet reluctant to miss even a syllable of his profound recollections.

Khan's tale paused, and for a breathless second, Jessie thought he might be finished. But his eyes gleamed with the promise of more—more secrets, more history, more connections to a world that until now had been just faded hieroglyphs in dusty textbooks.

"Go on," she urged, her voice tinged with both eagerness and affection for the enigmatic creature who shared her love of the esoteric. "I'm ready to travel further down this river of yours, Khan."

With a soft purr that seemed to acknowledge their unique partnership, Khan obliged, drawing Jessie deeper into the mysteries of his ancient homeland.

The air in Jessie's office began to pulse with a strange rhythm, as if it were breathing in time with Khan's narrative. The light bulb overhead flickered erratically, casting undulating shadows that twisted along the walls like otherworldly hieroglyphs come to life. Jessie felt an odd tingling at the back of her neck, and she instinctively reached up to rub it, her skin prickling with the sensation of invisible fingers tracing a path down her spine.

"Jessie," Khan's voice resonated with a depth that seemed to vibrate through the very floorboards, "in those days, I was more than just a silent watcher. I served as a vessel, a bridge for the gods to touch the world of mortals."

Jessie watched, spellbound, as the cat's emerald eyes held a seriousness that belied his usually snarky disposition. There was no mistaking the reverence in his tone, and she leaned in closer, her hazel eyes reflecting the strange dance of light and shadow around them.

"Secret chambers lay beneath the sand, hidden from the uninitiated," he continued, his gaze never leaving Jessie's. "There, the priests would gather, their voices low as they invoked ancient powers. They drew upon symbols and rites older than the pyramids themselves."

As Khan spoke, the images he conjured seemed to manifest in the air between them. Jessie could almost see the flicker of torchlight against stone walls, the air heavy with the scent of myrrh and frankincense. Hieroglyphs and symbols swirled in the semi-darkness, forming patterns that Jessie felt she should recognise, even though she knew she'd never seen them before.

"Each symbol was a key, each chant a step on a staircase leading to realms beyond our understanding," Khan explained, his tail flicking with a nonchalance that directly contradicted the gravity of his words.

Jessie nodded slowly, her mind a whirlwind of thoughts. She had always known there was more to her feline friend than met the eye, but this... this was beyond anything she could have imagined. Her breath caught in her throat as she watched the spectral symbols dance, her scholarly curiosity now mixed with a sense of wonder that bordered on the spiritual.

"Khan, this is..." Jessie struggled to find the words, her usual articulate nature failing her.

"History, Jessie. My history," Khan replied, his voice softening ever so slightly. "And perhaps, in some small way, yours as well."

Jessie's heart raced as the essence of Khan's tale swept her away, the boundaries of time and space blurring. She was no longer merely seated in the familiar confines of the Dale Street Private Investigations Agency; she was a spectator to an epoch long past. The scent of burning incense seemed to waft through the room, thick and aromatic, transporting her senses to the bustling banks of the ancient Nile.

"Can you hear them, Jessie?" Khan's voice was a whisper, yet it echoed with the resonance of ages. "The priests, their chants weaving through the air like the sacred serpents of protection."

She could, indeed. The low, rhythmic intonations, distant yet unmistakeable, hummed in her ears, a haunting melody that resonated with the very core of her being. Her fingers twitched, itching for the comforting feel of pen on paper, to document the indescribable experience that unfolded before her.

"Khan," Jessie murmured, her eyes wide with amazement, "it's as if I'm standing right there amidst the pyramids."

His whiskers twitched in amusement. "Close your eyes, and you'll see even more."

As she complied, Jessie felt the last remnants of the ordinary world slip away. The worn leather armrests faded from beneath her hands, replaced by the ephemeral touch of desert winds that spoke of secrets in a language only her soul understood.

"Your wisdom," she began, opening her eyes to find Khan's gaze fixed upon her, "it's like an endless library, each story a volume of untold mysteries."

"Libraries are your territory," Khan replied, his tone laced with his characteristic snarkiness. "Consider me a living archive of the mysterious."

Jessie chuckled softly, recognising the affection behind his words. It was true; she had always been the one to delve into dusty tomes and decode cryptic texts. Yet here was Khan, embodying the knowledge she so cherished, a bridge to marvels beyond her wildest librarian dreams.

"Immense significance" hardly did justice to the being that now sat before her, tail curling with casual elegance. Khan was not just a clever cat with an uncanny ability to communicate. He was a custodian of history, a guardian of truths that transcended the mundane world she knew.

"Khan, I..." Jessie struggled to articulate the shift in her perception. This transformation from companion to celestial sentinel was as jarring as it was enlightening.

"Save your words, Jessie." Khan's eyes glinted with a knowing look. "There'll be plenty of time for talking. For now, just accept that some things in life—and beyond—are grander than they appear."

With a nod, Jessie leaned back, allowing herself to absorb the revelation. Khan was more than just her partner in paranormal investigations; he was a gateway to understanding the fabric of reality itself. And as she took a deep breath, grounding herself in the recent knowledge, she realised their adventures were only just beginning.

Khan's narrative trailed off into a moment of stillness, the air in the office thick with anticipation. Jessie watched as his eyes began to glow, the green hue taking on an otherworldly luminescence that seemed to cut through the centuries like a beacon. She held her breath, a shiver of excitement tinged with reverence tracing its way down her spine. It was clear the climax of his extraordinary tale was upon them.

"Prepare yourself, Jessie," Khan's voice resonated with an ancient power, "for the mere edge of what once was."

With a grace born of countless aeons, Khan stretched forth a paw, and the room itself responded. From the tips of his sleek black fur emerged spectral images that twined through the air like ethereal serpents. A procession of ghostly figures marched along the walls, their outlines shimmering with a brilliance that defied time. Hieroglyphs floated from the desk, spinning and weaving around Jessie, telling tales of a world long lost to sand and stars.

"Is this...?" Jessie couldn't finish her sentence, her gaze transfixed by the dance of ancient magic unfurling before her eyes.

"Indeed," Khan purred, a note of pride threading through the timbre of his voice. "A glimmer of the old kingdom's heart, the cradle of our shared past."

Jessie's eyes widened as she took it all in, the dim office now a stage for phantoms of history. The air hummed with energy, the taste of it metallic and sharp on her tongue. She could feel the passage of millennia in every flicker of light, every whisper of displaced air. The forgotten scent of myrrh and frankincense seemed to waft from the corners of the room, and she half-expected to hear the soft padding of sandals on stone.

"By the Great Library of Alexandria, this is incredible," Jessie murmured with a wit-sharpened wonder, her librarian's heart beating a tattoo against her ribs. It wasn't everyday one's partner turned out to be a conduit for the divine, much less put on a display that would astound Cecil B. DeMille, the Hollywood epic film director, leaving him green with envy.

"Merely a party trick," Khan said dismissively, though his chest puffed up slightly with feline satisfaction at her astounded reaction. But even as the last of the apparitions faded, Jessie knew that 'mere' was no longer a word that could apply to anything about Khan.

The office settled back into its mundane shape, the shadows retreating to their proper places, but the echo of power lingered, as did the newfound depth of their partnership. Jessie leaned back in her chair, her mind buzzing with the revelations and her notebook open and ready to capture the essence of the magic she had just witnessed. With a pen poised over paper, she realised the world just got a whole lot more interesting—and she wouldn't have it any other way.

The last of the ethereal wisps dissolved into the air, a final glimmer of ancient power winking out like a snuffed candle. Jessie's eyes remained fixed on the spot where phantoms had pirouetted only moments before, the remnants of magic still crackling faintly in her ears. She sank deeper into the embrace of her chair, the worn leather suddenly feeling more like a sanctuary than mere furniture.

"Khan," she began, her voice a whisper of wonder, "that was... I have no words."

"Words are overrated anyway," Khan replied, his tone lightening as he settled back onto his haunches, his tail wrapping around him like a velvet rope. "Actions speak volumes, do they not?"

The corner of Jessie's mouth twitched upward in an amused smile, despite the whirlwind that was her thoughts. She studied Khan, noting the way the light caught the subtle shimmer of his black fur. He was so much more than just a talking cat; he was a guardian of secrets, a keeper of history, and now, her closest confidante.

"Your loyalty," she said, finally finding her voice again. "It means everything. And to think, you were once perched on top of a bookshelf, watching me sort through late returns."

"Ah, those were the days," Khan mused with a mock sigh, though the twinkle in his emerald eyes betrayed his contentment. "But we've traded dusty shelves for dusty mysteries. A fair exchange, I'd say."

Jessie nodded, her heart swelling with affection for her feline friend. They had indeed come a long way from their quiet existence among the stacks of a Liverpool library. Now, amidst the seemingly ever-present fog that caressed the office windows, they shared a bond unbreakable by time or trials.

"Where we go from here, Khan," Jessie mused, her fingers absently tracing the edges of her journal, "the possibilities are endless."

"Indeed," Khan agreed, his voice rich with the promise of adventures yet to come. "But wherever it is, we go together. You and I, Jessie, against the world. No one else must know about these revelations. Not George, nor Bill. No one, my dear."

"Against the paranormal world, you mean," Jessie corrected with a grin, closing her journal with a soft snap, "and I will say nothing."

"Semantics," Khan quipped, flicking an ear dismissively. But his gaze held hers with a depth that transcended words, and Jessie felt the truth of their partnership resonate within her soul.

"Time to put this newfound knowledge to use, wouldn't you say?" Jessie suggested, her spirits rising with a desire to delve deeper into the mysteries that awaited them.

"Lead the way, my wise librarian," Khan purred, jumping down from the desk with a grace that belied the power he contained. "I'm right behind you."

As Jessie picked up her pen to jot down the last of her notes, the office felt charged with potential, the mundane world outside its walls now tinged with the possibility of magic at every corner. With Khan at her side, Jessie Harper was ready to turn the page to the next chapter of their extraordinary tale.

Jessie inhaled deeply, her chest expanding with both the air and the possibilities that now lay before her. She peered through the window at the dissipating fog, as if the lifting mist was a metaphor for the clarity she sought. In the wake of Khan's revelation, the world felt brimming with enigmas yet to be decoded, each more tantalising than the last.

"Khan," she began, her eyes giving the clue to the passion of an idea, "do you realise what this means? There are layers to our reality that we've only just begun to scratch."

"Scratching surfaces is one of my numerous talents," Khan replied, his tail curling around himself as he settled beside her journal. His tone was playfully snarky but Jessie knew that was a ploy to disguise the seriousness of what he had shown her.

"Layers upon layers," Jessie murmured, more to herself than to Khan, her mind weaving through the tapestry of mysteries that beckoned them. The office, once so familiar, now seemed like a launching pad into the unknown.

"Like lasagna, Jessie. A most delightful human invention," Khan offered, breaking her contemplation with his culinary comparison.

"Only you could compare the paranormal to pasta," Jessie chuckled, the sound light and airy in the room charged with potential.

"Both complex, layered, and infinitely satisfying," Khan quipped, his eyes sparkling with mirth.

Their laughter mingled for a moment before silence reclaimed the space, allowing the gravity of their situation to resume. Jessie's gaze met Khan's, and in that silent exchange, there was an unspoken understanding. They were partners not just in proximity but in purpose.

"Whatever comes next, we're in it together," Jessie affirmed, her voice steady despite the quiver of excitement that threatened to break through.

"Always," Khan replied, the warmth in his voice wrapping around Jessie like a comforting embrace.

As the fog outside cleared, revealing the bustling outlines of Dale Street, Jessie stood up from her chair. She smoothed her hair back from her face, ready to step into whatever strange new chapter awaited them. But for now... it could wait.

Jessie settled back into her chair, a journal open before her on the desk. The pen in her hand danced across the paper, sketching out words that barely seemed adequate to describe the cosmic saga Khan had just unfurled. The scratch of pen on parchment was rhythmic, almost hypnotic, as she attempted to distil the essence of what she'd learned into ink and fibre.

"Pyramids... Nile... ancient deities," she mumbled under her breath, her eyes flicking up to meet Khan's emerald stare. "How does one even begin to summarise a tale spun from the threads of time itself?"

"Carefully, and with a generous amount of flair," Khan replied, his tone dripping with the snarkiness that Jessie found both infuriating and endearing.

The office around them seemed to buzz with an energy that defied explanation. Shadows played across the walls, no longer merely darkness chased by light but remnants of magic that had lingered, reluctant to return to whatever realm they had come from. Each flicker seemed to murmur secrets, beckoning Jessie to keep writing, to keep searching for truths veiled in mystery.

"Flair I can manage," Jessie said with a chuckle, her pen pausing as she glanced around at the transformed space. "But how do you footnote a supernatural event?"

"Ah, the eternal quandary of the paranormal investigator," Khan mused, circling comfortably on the desk before settling down like a sphinx guarding mysteries of old.

"Footnotes or not, I think we're onto something extraordinary," Jessie continued, feeling the importance of these discoveries settle around her like a cloak. Her fingers tapped the journal, each tap punctuating the gravity of their situation. "We've got a genuine enigma wrapped in a riddle here."

"Enigmas and riddles are my speciality," Khan quipped, his tail flicking with amusement. "Though I must admit, this is one for the ages."

With a final flourish, Jessie closed the journal, her notes a testament to the incredible story that had been shared. She looked around the once drab office, now alight with the glow of potential, and felt a thrill run through her. The line between the ordinary and the paranormal had been irrevocably blurred, and there was no turning back.

"Time to turn the page, then?" Jessie asked, her voice vibrant with the promise of adventure.

"Indeed," Khan purred contentedly. "After all, every good mystery needs its sleuths."

The warm atmosphere of the agency seemed to embrace them, the very air charged with the magic of possibility. Together, Jessie Harper and her enigmatic feline companion, Khan, were poised at the edge of the unknown, ready to leap into the next chapter of their uncanny journey.

Chapter Four

ADAPTING TO THE IMPOSSIBLE

IT WAS LATE IN the afternoon when Jessie Harper sat at her desk, the soft glow from the lone desk lamp casting long shadows across the cluttered room. She tapped her pencil against the notepad rhythmically, as if the beat could somehow help make sense of yesterday and Khan's extraordinary revelation. His true nature was not just a figment of myth or legend; it was real, and it had chosen to curl up on her windowsill.

"Your mind is racing like a greyhound after a mechanical rabbit," Khan observed with a snarky purr. The short black fur on his back bristled slightly in the dim light, and even though he sat perfectly still, there was an energy about him that seemed to pulse with ancient secrets.

Jessie glanced up, her eyes reflecting her feelings - a mix of incredulity and fond exasperation. "You'd think after all this time, you'd give me a break," she retorted, a small chuckle escaping her lips despite the whirlwind of thoughts. Her auburn hair fell in a loose wave over one shoulder, momentarily distracting her from the conversation.

"Ah, but where would be the fun in that?" Khan stretched languidly, his eyes gleaming with mischief. "Humans have such delightfully complex brains – all that capacity for wonder and yet, you're staggered by the thought of a talking cat."

"Correction: a magical talking cat, who apparently has been around since the pyramids were young," Jessie corrected, setting her pencil down and leaning back in her chair. She studied Khan's sleek form, the way his eyes seemed to hold centuries of wisdom and a hint of starlight. "It's not every day your feline friend turns out to be a relic of ancient history."

"Relic? I'm as spry as ever," Khan huffed, though the twinkle in his eye belied any offence. "Besides, we've more important things than my ageless charm. There are mysteries afoot, and we've never shied away from a good enigma."

Jessie's smile grew at that, the familiar thrill of the chase starting to cut through her initial shock. With Khan by her side, she felt ready to unravel any supernatural puzzle that came their way, no matter how steeped in antiquity or cloaked in shadow.

The shrill ring of the telephone sliced through the quietude of the dim office, startling Jessie from her thoughts. She jabbed at the pencil on her notepad one final time before reaching for the handset, the unexpected sound tethering her back to reality.

"Jessie Harper, Dale Street Private Investigations Agency," she answered, her voice steady despite the lingering haze in her mind.

"Miss Harper, it's Alf from the Curiosity Shoppe in Moorfields, just around the corner. I need your eyes on something peculiar," came the anxious reply, barely concealing a tremor. "There are markings on my shop walls, symbols that weren't there yesterday."

Jessie perked up immediately, her librarian's curiosity piqued by the mention of strange symbols. "I'll be right over, Alf. Try not to touch anything until I get there," she instructed, already imagining dusty tomes filled with arcane knowledge that might shed light on the mystery.

She hung up and turned to Khan, who had been pretending not to eavesdrop but betrayed himself with the flick of his tail. Their eyes met, shared excitement dancing in their gazes. "Looks like we've got a fresh puzzle on our hands," Jessie said, a smile spreading across her face.

"Indeed, the game is afoot," Khan intoned, his voice rich with anticipation. His snarky edge was softened by the affection he held for his human companion and their shared love of the otherworldly.

Jessie grabbed her well-worn coat from the back of her chair. "Ready for another adventure, Khan?"

"Always," Khan replied, his silhouette outlined by the moonlight spilling through the window. With a graceful bound that defied his ageless years, he leapt from his perch on the windowsill and padded toward the door, ready to weave once more into the fabric of the winter's evening alongside Jessie.

"Let's go unravel some ancient secrets," Jessie declared, her eyes alight with the thrill of discovery as she opened the door. The pair stepped out, leaving behind the stillness of the office for the promise of the unknown that awaited them in the Liverpool evening.

Liverpool embraced Jessie and Khan with a clammy hug as they emerged onto the fog-cloaked streets. A chill threaded through the air, creeping under Jessie's coat and drawing an involuntary shiver from her. The city was a symphony of muffled sounds—a car horn sounding in the distance, likewise a tram bell, a foghorn on the river and the occasional murmur of pedestrians wrapped up in their own worlds.

"Could do with a bit less of the damp," Jessie muttered, tugging her coat tighter around herself. She glanced down at Khan, his black fur almost a shadow against the wet paving stones, save for the spectral gleam of his alert green eyes.

"Ah, but mysteries are best served cold," Khan quipped, his voice no more than a whisper to avoid startling any passersby who might not appreciate a talking cat.

Jessie couldn't help but smile at his dry humour. "And here I thought you'd prefer the warmth of Egypt."

"Contrary to popular belief, a touch of English chill sharpens the senses," he retorted, tail swishing behind him as they navigated through the spectral veil of fog.

The shop came into view, its windows dark, but for the faint flicker of a blue beacon atop a Liverpool police car parked outside. They entered, but first, Khan made himself invisible to all save for Jessie. She had become used to Khan deploying that tactic. The symbols sprawled across the walls immediately drew Jessie's attention. A strange sense of familiarity tugged at her, her librarian instincts buzzing like a dormant engine suddenly roaring to life.

"Curiouser and curiouser," she murmured, pulling a notepad from her bag. Her hand moved of its own accord, jotting down notes, her thoughts racing to place each stroke and curve of the hieroglyphs into some semblance of meaning.

"Looks like something straight out of 'The Mummy's Curse,'" Khan observed, but now communicating telepathically with Jessie.

"Or the local prankster's guidebook," Jessie replied using the same telepathic channel, though her tone suggested she believed otherwise. The symbols had an authenticity that pricked at her academic curiosity—each one meticulously drawn, and appearing to resonate with an ancient pulse that even the most gifted forger would struggle to replicate.

"Let's see if we can find a pattern," Jessie said. She traced the lines of the hieroglyphs with her finger, each symbol igniting a spark of recognition as she delved deeper into the mystery before them.

Jessie's pencil tapped a steady rhythm against the notepad as her eyes darted between the symbols and her scrawled notes. Khan, invisible to all except Jessie, lent his mystical expertise to the analysis.

"Ah, you see this one?" he purred telepathically, his eyes catching a flicker of light as he pointed a paw at an intricate symbol. "That's the Eye of Horus; it's meant to protect against evil spirits—very popular in the old days."

"Old days for you being what? A couple thousand years ago?" Jessie teased, though she couldn't hide her fascination with the symbol's fine lines.

"Give or take a few centuries," Khan replied with a snarky smirk. "But let's not forget this one," he continued, motioning towards another glyph. "It represents Anubis, the god of embalming and the dead. Could be our vandals are trying to invoke something quite... ancient."

His voice trailed off as the front door creaked open, admitting a uniformed police constable whose sceptical frown seemed carved into his face like the symbols on the wall. He surveyed the scene, disbelief showing in his furrowed brow.

"Evening, constable," Jessie said, her tone the epitome of calm despite the absurdity of the situation. "I believe these might be more than just random acts of vandalism. There seems to be a purpose behind the hieroglyphs, possibly tied to ancient rituals."

The officer raised an eyebrow. "Ancient rituals? In Liverpool?" He scoffed lightly, but struggled to hide his curiosity.

"Quite so," Jessie affirmed, her eyes meeting his with quiet confidence. "Each symbol here carries historical significance. If we understand their meaning, we might get to the bottom of why they've appeared."

Khan, still invisible and now sitting inconspicuously atop a nearby shelf, watched the exchange with a concealed grin. The disbelief of the officer was almost comical to him, a being who'd walked the sands of time when these symbols were first carved into stone.

"Alright then, Miss Harper," the police constable said after a moment, clearly deciding to entertain the notion. "We'll leave you to it. But do keep us posted on any... breakthroughs in your... investigation."

As the officer left, Jessie turned back to the wall, her mind already racing with possibilities. Khan leapt down from his perch, his presence a silent vow that they would unravel this enigma, one hieroglyph at a time.

Stepping out of the shop into the brisk evening air, Jessie buttoned her coat up to her chin, while Khan trotted alongside. The dim glow from the streetlamps cast long shadows across the pavement as they navigated through the narrow alleyways leading back to Dale Street.

"Can you believe that constable?" Jessie mused, a smirk playing on her lips. "I thought his moustache was going to jump off his face when I mentioned ancient rituals."

"Human disbelief is as constant as the North Star," Khan replied, his eyes flickering with mischief. "But then again, who needs their conviction when we have truth on our side?" He leapt onto a low wall, balancing with feline grace.

Their chuckles were interrupted by hushed tones floating from a knot of dock workers gathered outside a pub. One, a burly man with tattooed forearms, crossed himself and glanced nervously at the shop they'd just left.

"Mark my words, it's curses that befall us," he muttered. "Ancient spells woven into the very walls."

Jessie approached them, adopting her professional manner and softening into the warm, reassuring presence she was known for. "No curses here, gentlemen. Just some history trying to speak to us, that's all."

"History doesn't usually scare the living daylights out of you, Miss Harper," another docker with a battered flat cap chimed in, his eyes wide.

"It's only scary if you let it," Jessie replied, flashing a comforting smile that seemed to ease their tension. She peered closely at the man with the flat cap and said, "How is it you know my name, may I ask?"

"You and Mister Jenkins spoke to me about that cold case murder on the docks. It was nearly Christmas a few years back.

"Ah, yes, I remember now," Jessie said.

From his elevated position, Khan gave the dockers a sly wink before jumping down, causing a few surprised gasps before laughter broke through their unease. "See? Even the cat isn't worried," one worker chuckled, rubbing Khan's head as he passed by.

Jessie waited until out of earshot of the dockers before speaking. "Come on, Khan. We've got a trail to follow," she said, turning her attention back to the task at hand. She pulled out her notepad and pencil, scanning the buildings for more of the enigmatic symbols.

"Lead the way, sleuth extraordinaire," Khan said with an exaggerated bow before sauntering ahead.

They wound their way deeper into Liverpool's city centre, where every corner whispered tales of the past. Jessie's mind worked like clockwork, piecing together the puzzle with each new hieroglyph they found. Her notes became a map of conjectures and historical intersections, the lead of her pencil dancing fervently across the page.

"Ah, look at this one," she exclaimed, pointing to a symbol etched discreetly on a brick wall. "It's the Eye of Horus. Protection, royal power, good health."

"Or someone has a flair for dramatic irony," Khan commented dryly, his tail twitching with amusement.

"Either way," Jessie said in excitement, "it feels like we're on the right path."

"Indeed," Khan agreed, his silhouette sleek against the emerging moonlight. "And with every step, the story unfolds."

As they traced the mysterious inscriptions, Jessie's confidence swelled. Every hieroglyph whispered secrets of a time long forgotten but she felt invincible in her pursuit of the truth, especially so with Khan by her side. Together, they moved through the city, the night alive with the promise of revelation.

Navigating the labyrinthine streets, Jessie and Khan arrived at a crossroad that seemed to hum with an ancient energy. The fog had now returned drifting in from the river. It hugged the ground, creating a carpet soft as whispers underfoot. A chill wind danced through the air, carrying with it the faintest hint of incense and something far more arcane. Jessie thought it was unusual to feel a wind when it's foggy. Her thoughts were broken by Khan.

"Getting warmer," Khan murmured, his voice a velvety purr in the cool night. With the grace of a shadow, he slipped into an alleyway, the solitary streetlamp reflecting off his glossy black coat in fleeting silver strokes.

"Wait for me," Jessie said, her breath forming small clouds as she followed. She clutched her notepad close against her chest. Khan's occasional disappearance into the darkened nooks of Liverpool was both eerie and reassuring; his stealth was a cloak they both wore against prying eyes.

"Always," came his muffled reply from the darkness ahead.

They emerged onto the very dockyard where she and George had questioned the flat-capped docker. The silhouette of an old warehouse loomed like a forgotten monolith. Its windows were dark, the once sturdy doors now gaping, inviting secrets and intruders alike. Khan reappeared, sitting nonchalantly beside a rusted barrel, his green eyes scanning the area before looking at Jessie.

"Through there," he nodded towards the entrance, a silent signal that the game was afoot.

Jessie trod carefully over the uneven ground, the scent of brine and decay strong in her nostrils. Inside the warehouse, shadows clung to every corner, but there was movement too—subtle and rhythmic. Candles flickered, casting elongated figures against the walls, and low chants echoed off the high ceilings.

"Are those...?" Jessie started, peering closer at the group gathered in a circle.

"Ritualists," Khan confirmed, his tone grave yet tinged with excitement. "And they're not here for knitting."

"Looks like we found your cultists," Jessie whispered, her words a mix of dread and determination. She could feel the thrum of power in the air, a tangible vibration that set her nerves on edge.

"Or they've found us," Khan replied, his whiskers twitching in the candlelight. They shared a look, a silent conversation passing between them. There was danger here, but also opportunity—the chance to stop whatever madness was about to unfold.

With careful steps, they crept closer, staying hidden behind crates stamped with forgotten destinations. The chanting grew louder, more insistent, as if the very words could tear the veil between worlds. Jessie's hand went to her throat, feeling the thump of her heart against her fingers.

"Ready, Jessie?" Khan asked, his feline form coiled and ready to spring.

"Not really but let's do this," she answered, her voice steady despite the chaos brewing before them. Together, they watched, waited, and prepared to act. The bond between them—a librarian turned sleuth and her enigmatic, magical cat—never felt stronger. This was their moment to face the unknown and emerge victorious.

Jessie's eyes darted from symbol to symbol, her mind racing through the esoteric knowledge she'd acquired over years of poring over ancient texts. Each hieroglyph was a piece of a larger puzzle—a forbidden summoning that could not be completed. "Khan, create a diversion," she whispered, her voice a hushed command.

"Diversion?" Khan's snarky tone cut through the tension. "I thought you'd never ask." In a flash of black fur, he sprang into action, toppling a stack of crates with a precision that sent them crashing down like dominoes.

The cultists jerked around, their chant stumbling into silence as chaos erupted. Some scurried towards the noise, while others looked on in bewilderment, their focus shattered.

Seizing the moment, Jessie moved swiftly. She reached for the central artefact, a stone tablet etched with the most potent of the glyphs, and began to carefully, but firmly, scrape away at its surface with a small tool from her coat pocket. Her hands were steady, betraying none of the adrenaline that coursed through her veins.

"Looking for this?" Khan's voice rang out, dripping with mischief as he batted a ceremonial dagger away from the grasping hands of a robed figure. The cultist stumbled, tripping over Khan's sleek, darting form.

"Nice work," Jessie called out, her focus undiminished even as she acknowledged his efforts. Her fingers traced the contours of the symbols, each line disrupted weakening the fabric of the ritual.

"Always happy to serve," Khan quipped, his green eyes glinting with delight beneath the flickering candlelight. He weaved through the confusion he'd sown, a shadow of deft movements and cunning distractions.

The air within the warehouse seemed to pulse with thwarted energy, a crackling tension that hovered just on the brink of release. Jessie felt it prickling at her skin, a reminder of the danger they narrowly skirted.

"Almost there," she murmured, her breath visible in the cold air as she worked to erase the last symbol. With a final stroke, the glyph was rendered incomplete, its power dissipating into the ether. The room quietened, the residual magic fizzling out like a snuffed candle.

"Oops," Khan said, feigning innocence as he watched the last of the cultists flee, their dreams of awakening ancient powers dashed by a librarian and a cat.

Together, Jessie and Khan turned their attention to dismantling the rest of the ritual setup. Candles were snuffed out, incense sticks crushed underfoot, and every trace of the occult gathering swept away as if it had never been.

"Another close call," Jessie sighed, tucking her hair behind her ear as she surveyed their handiwork.

"Close? Please, we had it under control," Khan's voice was a mix of pride and fondness as he rubbed against her leg. "After all, what's an ancient Egyptian cat god for, if not a little excitement?"

The two shared a knowing smile, their bond unspoken but deeply felt as they stepped out of the warehouse, leaving the remnants of the night's ordeal behind them.

The fog clung to the streets of Liverpool like a spectral blanket, but as Jessie and Khan made their way back to their dimly lit office, it seemed to retreat, as if cowed by their victory. Jessie's boots clicked rhythmically against the pavement, keeping time with Khan's silent, feline tread.

"Looks like we're in for a clear morning," Jessie observed, pulling her coat tighter around her. The chill had sunk into her bones during the night's escapade, but the thought of a warm cup of tea was already coaxing a smile onto her lips.

"Clear skies are overrated," Khan quipped, his tail flickering with a contented swagger. "Give me a good shroud of mystery any day."

They ascended the steps to their office, the familiar creak of the door welcoming them back to their sanctuary. Inside, Jessie flicked on the lamp, bathing the room in a soft, golden glow. She sank into her chair with a satisfied sigh, while Khan leapt onto the windowsill, his green eyes reflecting the first tentative rays of dawn.

"Another case closed," Jessie said, allowing herself a moment to bask in the quiet triumph. "What would I do without you?"

"Probably live a very boring life," Khan replied, his tone light but sincere. "But let's not find out."

Jessie chuckled as her eyes locked onto Khan's. There was a warmth there, a depth of gratitude for the enigmatic feline who had become her closest companion and confidant.

"Indeed." She stood up, stretching her arms above her head. "Now, how about that breakfast I promised? I believe you've earned your choice of fish from the market."

"Salmon," Khan declared without hesitation. "And make it a double portion."

"Greedy cat," Jessie teased, but her affectionate tone betrayed her indulgence. She grabbed her keys, ready to step out once more, when she noticed the notes they'd taken earlier scattered across her desk. Hieroglyphs, ancient rituals, and now a trail of new questions unfurling before them.

"More mysteries await," Jessie mused, her mind already turning over the possibilities.

"Let them come," Khan said, jumping down to accompany her. "After all, what is life without a little enchantment?"

Arm in arm, or rather hand by paw, Jessie and Khan left their office, stepping out into the burgeoning daylight. The fog had lifted entirely now, revealing the city anew—a city that held secrets only they could unravel. And together, they were more than ready to meet whatever lay ahead.

Chapter Five

SHADOWS OF THE PAST

THE SAME DAY

Breakfast of poached salmon for Khan and poached eggs on toast for Jessie was over and the two sleuths napped for a few hours catching up on sleep lost the night before.

Some hours later, Jessie saw that the fog had returned. It swirled outside the grimy office window, distorting the shadows into eerie shapes that danced along the wall. In the dim light, Jessie Harper leaned forward, her eyes sparkling with curiosity as they met the emerald gaze of her feline companion. Khan sat perched on the edge of the desk, his black fur shimmering faintly in the gloom.

"Khan," Jessie began, "I think it's time you told me more about your past. I feel like I barely know anything about your life before we met." She absently twirled a lock of auburn hair around her finger.

The cat flicked his tail thoughtfully, considering her request. After a moment, he inclined his head. "Very well, Jessie. I suppose you've earned the right to know more, given all we've been through together."

Khan shifted on the desk, his lithe form somehow commanding attention even in the cluttered office. His eyes seemed to glow with an inner light as they locked onto

Jessie's. When he spoke, his voice sounded different... disengaged.

"My story begins long ago, in the distant lands of Egypt, during an age when gods walked among mortals and magic thrummed in the very air." His tone was mesmerising, drawing Jessie in.

She leaned closer, barely breathing, as if the slightest sound might break the spell. This is it, she thought. Finally, a glimpse behind the enigmatic feline's facade. Her heart raced with anticipation.

Khan's whiskers twitched, a faint smile playing about his muzzle. "Ah, but where to begin? So many tales, so many lives entwined with the sands of time." His eyes took on a faraway look as the memories washed over him.

As Khan began to recount his extraordinary past, Jessie felt the world around her start to fade away, replaced by the vivid images conjured by the cat's hypnotic words. She knew instinctively that nothing would ever be the same again. The mysteries Khan guarded were about to be unveiled, and she could only hope she was ready for the revelations to come.

As Khan's tale unfolded, the air in the room began to shimmer and pulse with an otherworldly energy. Jessie blinked, her eyes widening as the walls of their office gradually dissolved, replaced by the sprawling sands and towering pyramids of ancient Egypt. The transformation was so seamless, so enchanting, that she couldn't help but gasp in wonder.

"By the gods," she breathed, her voice barely above a whisper. "It's... it's incredible."

Khan's tail swished with satisfaction, a knowing glint in his eyes. "Ah, but this is merely a glimpse, my dear Jessie. A window into a world long past, but never truly forgotten."

Jessie stood, her legs carrying her forward as if drawn by an invisible force. The sand beneath her feet felt warm and real, the grains shifting with each step. She marvelled at the sight of grand temples adorned with hieroglyphs, their golden surfaces gleaming under the eternal sun. In the distance, the bustling sounds of a marketplace drifted on the breeze, mingling with the distant chant of priests.

The scent of exotic incense filled the air, wrapping around her like an intoxicating embrace. Jessie felt her heart swell with a profound sense of connection, as though she had stepped into a living tapestry of history. Every sight, every sound, every sensation was a thread woven into the rich fabric of Khan's memories.

"I never imagined..." she whispered, her voice thick with emotion. "It's like I'm really here, standing in the very heart of ancient Egypt."

Khan padded silently to her side, his presence a comforting anchor in the midst of the extraordinary. "In a way, you are," he purred, his voice a soothing rumble. "This is the power of memory, Jessie. A magic that transcends time and space, allowing us to walk in the footsteps of the past."

Jessie reached out, her fingertips grazing the sun-warmed stone of a nearby obelisk. The surface thrummed with an ancient energy, sending a shiver down her spine. She knew, deep in her soul, that this was only the beginning of a journey that would change everything she thought she knew about the world - and about the enigmatic feline by her side.

As the vision shimmered and shifted, the bustling marketplace faded away, replaced by the grandeur of a royal palace. Jessie found herself standing in a vast hall, its walls adorned with intricate hieroglyphs and vibrant frescoes. At the far end, seated upon a magnificent throne, was a woman whose beauty and presence seemed to command the very air itself.

"Cleopatra," Khan murmured, his feline eyes glinting with admiration. "Queen of the Nile, and one of the most remarkable figures in all of history."

Jessie watched in awe as Khan gracefully approached the throne, his sleek form moving with a fluid elegance that seemed to belong to another world. The courtiers and attendants parted before him, their faces a mix of reverence and wonder. Even Cleopatra herself seemed to sit up straighter, her regal gaze fixed upon the approaching feline.

"I remember the day I first met her," Khan continued, his voice low and rich with memory. "She was a woman of extraordinary intelligence and wit, with a heart as fierce as any warrior's."

As Khan spoke, the scene unfolded before Jessie's eyes. She saw Khan sitting at Cleopatra's feet, engaging in lively discussions of politics, philosophy, and the mysteries of the universe. The queen and the cat seemed to share a bond that transcended the boundaries of species and station, a connection forged in the crucible of a turbulent age.

"It was an honour to be her companion and advisor," Khan mused, his voice tinged with a hint of wistfulness. "To witness the making of history, and to play a small part in shaping its course."

The vision shifted once more, and Jessie found herself standing in the heart of a temple, the air heavy with the scent of incense. Khan stood before an altar, his form almost luminous in the flickering torchlight. Around him, priests and acolytes moved in solemn procession, their chants rising and falling like the breath of the gods themselves.

"In those days, I was more than just a cat," Khan explained, his voice echoing strangely in the sacred space. "I was a bridge between the mortal world and the divine, a conduit for the power that flowed through the very stones of the temple."

Jessie felt a shiver run down her spine as she watched Khan participate in the ancient rituals, his movements imbued with a grace and purpose that seemed to transcend the merely physical. She could almost feel the energy that pulsed through the temple, a tangible force that thrummed in her very bones.

"I never knew," she breathed, her eyes wide with wonder. "I mean, I always sensed there was something special about you, but this... it's beyond anything I could have imagined."

Khan turned to her, his eyes glowing with an inner light. "You and I, Jessie... we are part of something greater than ourselves. A story that has been unfolding for centuries, a tapestry woven from the threads of magic and mystery."

Jessie nodded, her heart swelling with a sense of purpose and destiny. She knew, with a certainty that defied explanation, that her path was intertwined with Khan's, and that together they would unravel the secrets of the past - and shape the course of the future.

As the vision began to fade, the temple walls dissolving into mist and memory, Jessie reached out and laid a hand on Khan's silken fur. "Thank you," she whispered, her voice thick with emotion. "For sharing this with me, for trusting me with your story."

Khan leaned into her touch, his purr a gentle rumble of affection and understanding. "Our story, Jessie," he corrected gently. "Our story."

As the last wisps of the vision dissipated, a sudden chill crept into the office, raising goosebumps on Jessie's skin. The air grew heavy, charged with an unseen presence that set her nerves on edge. Khan's ears twitched, his body tensing as he sensed the shift in the atmosphere.

"What is it?" Jessie whispered, "What's happening?"

Khan's eyes narrowed, his gaze darting around the room as if searching for an invisible threat. "We are not alone," he murmured, his voice low and urgent. "There are others here, drawn by the power of the memories we've unleashed."

Jessie swallowed hard, her mouth suddenly dry. "Others? You mean... other beings like you?"

The enigmatic feline nodded, his tail lashing in agitation. "Ancient ones, with their own agendas and desires. They sense the magic we've tapped into, and they want a piece of it for themselves."

A low rumble echoed through the office, like distant thunder on a stormy night. The walls began to tremble, and the floor beneath their feet vibrated with an ominous energy. Jessie's heart raced, her mind struggling to comprehend the enormity of what was happening.

"Khan, what do we do?" she asked, her voice trembling with a mix of fear and determination. "How do we stop this?"

The cat's eyes flashed with an otherworldly light, and he rose to his full height, his fur bristling with power.

"We stand our ground," he declared, his voice ringing with authority. "We show them that we are not to be trifled with, that our bond is stronger than any force they can muster."

As if in response to Khan's words, a swirling vortex of sand began to form in the centre of the room, growing larger and more violent with each passing second. The grains whipped through the air, stinging Jessie's skin and obscuring her vision. She squinted against the onslaught, her hand instinctively reaching out to grasp Khan's fur for support.

"Is that... a sandstorm?" she gasped, her words nearly lost in the howling wind. "Inside the office?"

Khan's eyes narrowed to slits, his body coiled with a primal readiness. "Not just any sandstorm," he growled, his voice barely audible over the roar of the wind. "A manifestation of a rival deity, a challenge to our connection and our power."

Jessie's heart thundered in her chest, her mind buzzing with the implications of Khan's words. She knew, with a bone-deep certainty, that this was a pivotal moment - a test of their bond, and of their ability to navigate the treacherous waters of the paranormal world they had plunged into.

As the sandstorm raged around them, obscuring the familiar contours of the office and plunging them into a world of swirling chaos, Jessie and Khan stood side by side, united in their determination to face whatever challenges lay ahead. The air crackled with ancient magic, and Jessie could feel the past, all of history from centuries past pressing down upon them - but she also felt the strength of their connection, the indestructible bond that had brought them together across the vast expanse of time and space.

"Together," she whispered, her fingers tightening in Khan's fur. "We'll face this together."

And as the storm intensified, as the very fabric of reality seemed to warp and twist around them, Jessie and Khan stood fast, ready to confront the unknown and emerge victorious on the other side.

Khan's eyes glowed with an ethereal light, his sleek form radiating an ancient power that sent shivers down Jessie's spine. He leapt forward, his paws barely touching the ground as he positioned himself between Jessie and the heart of the sandstorm. The air around him shimmered, his fur standing on end as he channelled the full might of his magic to counter the attack.

Jessie watched in awe as Khan stood firm, his tail lashing and his ears flattened against his head. The roar of the wind intensified, the sand whipping around them in a frenzied dance, but Khan remained unmoving, a bastion of strength during the chaos.

"Stay close to me, Jessie," Khan called out, his voice cutting through the howling gale. "I'll protect you."

Jessie nodded, her heart pounding with a mix of fear and admiration. She had always known that Khan was special, but seeing him like this - a true guardian, a being of immense power - left her breathless.

The sandstorm surged forward, the rival deity's energy clashing against Khan's in a dazzling display of light and sound. The room trembled, the walls groaning under the strain of the supernatural forces at play. Jessie clutched at Khan's fur, her eyes wide as she watched the battle unfold.

Khan's eyes narrowed, his whiskers twitching as he summoned every ounce of his strength. Ancient words spilled from his lips, a chant in a language long forgotten by mortals. The air around him pulsed with energy, and Jessie could feel the heat emanating from his body, a testament to the raw power coursing through his veins.

The clash of energies intensified, the sandstorm raging against Khan's unyielding presence. Jessie's heart raced, her breath coming in short gasps as she witnessed the incredible display of magic before her. She had never seen anything like it, and a part of her feared the consequences of tampering with such ancient forces.

Yet, even in the midst of the chaos, Jessie trusted Khan completely. She knew that he would do everything in his power to keep her safe, to protect the bond they had forged through their shared curiosity and determination.

As the battle raged on, Jessie closed her eyes, silently offering her own strength to Khan. She may not have possessed his magical abilities, but she believed in the power of their connection, in the unbreakable ties that bound them together.

And so, side by side, Jessie and Khan faced the sandstorm, their hearts beating as one as they fought to maintain the delicate balance between the mortal world and the realm of the divine.

With a final surge of power, Khan dispelled the storm, the sand dissipating into nothingness. The office returned to its familiar state, though the air still hummed with residual energy. The ancient Egyptian landscape faded away, replaced by the comforting sight of their cluttered desk and the soft glow of the desk lamp.

Jessie, breathless and wide-eyed, approached Khan, her mind racing with the implications of what she'd witnessed. She reached out, her fingers gently brushing against his shimmering black fur, marvelling at the power that lay beneath his feline exterior.

"Khan, that was..." Jessie struggled to find the right words, her voice filled with a mix of awe and gratitude. "I've never seen anything like it. Thank you for sharing that with me, for protecting us."

Khan turned to face her, his eyes softening as he met her gaze. "It's what I'm here for, Jessie. To guide you, to keep you safe as we unravel the mysteries of the paranormal world."

Jessie smiled, a sense of warmth spreading through her chest. "I'm just glad you're okay. For a moment there, I thought..."

She trailed off, the unspoken fear hanging in the air between them. Khan nuzzled his head against her hand, a gentle reminder of his presence. "I'm not going any-where, Jessie. We're in this together, no matter what."

Jessie nodded, her eyes shining with a renewed sense of purpose. She knew that their journey had only just begun, that there were countless secrets waiting to be uncovered. But with Khan by her side, she felt ready to face anything.

As the last traces of ancient magic faded from the room, Jessie and Khan shared a moment of quiet un-derstanding. The world outside their office may have been shrouded in fog and mystery, but together, they would illuminate the truth, one case at a time.

Jessie took a deep breath, the recent experience still on her mind. She turned to Khan, "What we just wi tnessed... it was incredible. But it also made me realise just how much there is that we don't know, how much power lies hidden in the world."

Khan nodded, his tail flicking thoughtfully as he considered her words. "You're right, Jessie. The secrets we seek are not to be taken lightly. We must tread carefully, always mindful of the forces we may unleash."

He leapt gracefully onto the desk, his black fur shimmering in the dim light of the office. "But remember, our bond is our greatest strength. As long as we trust in each other, we can face whatever challenges come our way."

Jessie reached out, gently scratching behind Khan's ears, a gesture of affection and gratitude. She marvelled at the softness of his fur, the warmth of his presence. In that moment, she knew that their partnership was more than just a quirky detective duo - it was a connection that transcended the boundaries of the ordinary world.

Reflecting on the experience, Jessie's mind raced with the implications of their journey. The knowledge she had gained, the wonders she had witnessed, they had forever changed her perception of reality. She knew that the path ahead would be fraught with danger, that the cost of uncovering the truth may be higher than she ever imagined.

But with Khan by her side, she felt a sense of purpose, a drive to unravel the mysteries that lay ahead. Together, they would step into the unknown, guided by their shared curiosity and a shatterproof bond.

Jessie looked out the window, the fog outside now seeming less ominous and more like a veil waiting to be lifted. She smiled, her hazel eyes sparkling with a sense of adventure. "Well, Khan," she said, her voice tinged with excitement, "I guess we'd better get ready. Something tells me this is just the beginning."

Khan purred in agreement, his green eyes glinting with a knowing look. "Indeed, Jessie. The mysteries that await us are as vast as the sands of Egypt. But together, we shall uncover them, one paw print at a time."

Jessie chuckled softly, reaching out to scratch Khan behind his ears. "One paw print at a time? I like the sound of that." She paused, her expression growing thoughtful. "You know, Khan, when I first started this journey, I had no idea where it would lead me. But now, with you by my side, I feel like anything is possible."

Khan leaned into her touch, his eyes closing in contentment. "Ah, my dear Jessie, that is the beauty of the unknown. It holds the promise of endless possibilities, of discoveries that can change the very fabric of our understanding." He opened his eyes, fixing her with a meaningful gaze. "And I couldn't ask for a better companion to explore those possibilities with."

Jessie felt a warmth radiate through her entire body, a sense of gratitude and affection for the enigmatic feline. She stood up, stretching her arms above her head. "Alright then, partner. Let's get to work. We've got a lot of research to do if we're going to unravel the secrets of your past and the mysteries that lie ahead."

Khan leapt gracefully from the desk, his tail swishing with anticipation. "Lead the way, Jessie. Together, we shall shine a light on the shadows and bring the truth to the surface."

Jessie paused looked at Khan, a smile playing on her lips. "You know, Khan, I have a feeling that this is going to be one heck of an adventure."

Khan's eyes glimmered with mischief. "Oh, Jessie, you have no idea. But that's what makes it so delightfully intriguing, doesn't it?"

With a shared laugh, they stepped out of the office, ready to face whatever challenges and mysteries the future held, their bond stronger than ever.

Chapter Six

THE AWAKENING

THE OFFICE HAD BEEN a cocoon of tranquillity, with the soft ticking of the clock and the shuffle of pages as Jessie Harper lost herself in ancient lore. That is until the world outside took a deep breath and exhaled a fog so dense it seemed to swallow the city whole. She paused, her finger tracing the line of text she'd been reading and turned to look out the window.

"Blimey," she murmured, her breath casting a ghostly cloud on the glass. "That's not natural."

Khan sat perched atop a stack of books, his shimmering black fur standing on end as if electrified by the strange atmosphere. His green eyes narrowed, and he let out a low, rumbling growl that vibrated through the silence.

"Indeed," Khan replied, his tone belying the unease that rippled through him. "It appears we're not in for an ordinary day."

As if on cue, the shrill ring of the telephone shattered the eerie calm. Jessie reached for the receiver, her movements quick and precise—a librarian turned sleuth, always ready for the unexpected. "Jessie Harper, how can I be of assistance?"

The voice on the other end was frantic, words tumbling over each other like dominoes in a storm. "Miss Harper, it's chaos here! Locusts, swarms of them, at the docks!" A dockworker, no doubt, terror seeping through the connection like water through cracks.

"Locusts?" Jessie echoed, her eyebrows knitting together in concentration. She scribbled notes in a leather-bound notebook that contained more secrets than the local library. "We'll be right there."

She hung up and swung into action, grabbing her coat with one hand and her trusty notebook with the other. Khan leapt from his literary throne, landing with feline grace onto Jessie's shoulder, his tail flicking with anticipation.

"Looks like we've got our work cut out for us," Jessie said, fastening the buttons of her coat with swift, determined motions.

"Ah, but when have we ever shied away from a challenge, dear Jessie?" Khan purred, his voice a comforting blend of affection and mischief. "After all, what is life without a little excitement?"

Jessie chuckled, the sound soft and light despite the situation. "You and your excitement, Khan. One of these days, it'll be the death of me."

"Perish the thought," Khan retorted, though his gaze remained fixed on the swirling mists outside. "I'd miss our delightful banter far too much."

They stepped from the safety of their office into the murky unknown, the door closing behind them with a resolute click. Ahead lay mystery and mayhem, but Jessie Harper and her magical talking cat were no strangers to the peculiar dance of danger. Together, they ventured forth, cloaked in camaraderie and armed with wit, wisdom, and a touch of the paranormal.

Jessie's steps were brisk, her boots thudding against the cobblestone as she wove through the shrouded alleyways of Liverpool. The fog, thick and relentless, clung to her like a second skin, but Jessie's memory was a trusty guide, painting a mental map of the streets she knew by heart. Khan, perched on her shoulder, kept his ears pricked for any discordant sound, his keen senses cutting through the peasouper with an ease that was almost supernatural.

"Left at the next junction," Khan murmured into her ear, his voice clear in the hush that enveloped them.

"Got it," Jessie replied, her voice steady despite the adrenaline that tingled in her veins. They turned the corner, and the distant drone of buzzing grew into a cacophony that sent a shiver down Jessie's spine. She couldn't see the swarm yet, but she could feel its chaotic pulse vibrating in the air, a harbinger of the pandemonium they were about to confront.

"Sounds like a proper insect orchestra, doesn't it?" Jessie quipped, trying to keep the mood light even as her grip tightened around the notebook that contained countless solutions for countless problems—though none quite like this.

"Indeed," Khan agreed, his tail twitching in disapproval. "Though I must say, I prefer a quiet evening by the fire with Vivaldi playing on the gramophone, not this...buz zing nightmare."

As they emerged from the fog onto the docks, the blanket of fog disappeared but the scene before them was one of utter bedlam. Locusts swarmed in thick clouds, a living, writhing veil that obscured the view of the River Mersey beyond. Dockworkers flailed their arms, swatting futilely at the relentless insects that invaded every nook and cranny, their panic as real as the mist that had followed Jessie and Khan from their office.

"Steady on, folks!" Jessie called out, her librarian's command grabbing the attention of a few startled workers. "Let's try to keep our heads while we sort this out!"

Khan surveyed the chaos with narrowed eyes, his feline grace undiminished by the disorder around them. He gave Jessie a nod, his green eyes glinting with resolve beneath the eerie half-light.

"Time to weave some magic, Jessie," he said, his tone serious now, all traces of snarkiness momentarily set aside. "We can't let this plague run rampant."

"Right behind you, Khan," Jessie affirmed, drawing strength from her companion's unwavering confidence. Together, they stepped deeper into the tumult, ready to face whatever force had unleashed this miniature apocalypse upon their beloved city.

Jessie's fingers raced through the well-worn pages of her notebook, the paper almost crinkling in protest as she searched for the particular incantation she knew was nestled amongst her meticulous notes. Khan perched on a nearby crate, his shimmering black fur stark against the chaos of the docks, tail flicking with a rhythm that only he understood.

"Ah, here it is," Jessie muttered under her breath, uncovering the scribbled words of an ancient Egyptian ritual that felt older than time itself. She glanced at Khan, who had closed his eyes, gathering the mystical energies that coursed through his being.

"Ready when you are," she said, clutching the notebook to her chest like a talisman.

Khan opened his eyes, and they glowed an other-worldly emerald in the gloom. He raised his head, and from deep within his chest, a chant began to resonate, ancient syllables weaving through the air, each one vibrating with power. The sound was primal and haunting, a language unheard by human ears for millennia.

As Khan's voice grew stronger, it seemed to ripple through the swarm of locusts, which started to falter in their frenzied dance. Dockworkers paused to cover their ears, unnerved by the sound but grateful for any respite from the winged onslaught.

"Good show, Khan," Jessie whispered, admiration lacing her voice as the thick cloud of insects began to thin out, spiralling skyward, disappearing into the low grey clouds that had hung over the city for days like a well-worn hat.

With the immediate threat dispersing, Jessie's gaze drifted towards the River Mersey, where a new horror awaited them. The water - usually a murky greyish brown - now ran red, the colour of rusted iron, staining the waves with an ominous tinge.

"Blood in the water," Jessie murmured, "that can't be good."

"Understatement of the century," Khan quipped, his snarky comments returning even as his chant tapered off. His eyes remained luminous, scanning the river-bank with an intensity that belied his relaxed posture.

Together, they made their way towards the crimson waters, each step purposeful yet cautious. The usually briny scent of the docklands was replaced with a metallic tang that set Jessie's teeth on edge. She resisted the urge to cover her nose; instead, she focused on the notepad still clutched in her hand, its pages fluttering in the breeze like the wings of the departing locusts.

"Looks like we're not done yet," Jessie said, more to herself than to Khan. But the enigmatic feline merely nodded, ready to face whatever lay ahead with his usual blend of mystique and sass.

"Never a dull moment with you, is there, Harper?" Khan remarked, his voice tinged with affection despite the dire circumstances.

"Nor with you, my friend," Jessie replied with a warm smile, her heart fortified by the bond they shared, a bond that would carry them through the maelstrom of magic and mystery that awaited them on the banks of the blood-red Mersey.

The coppery tang of the River Mersey filled Jessie's senses as she fumbled with the pages of her notebook, the delicate script of her notes blurring before her anxious eyes. Her hands trembled, not just from the chill in the air but from the challenge that lay before her.

"Come on, Jess," she murmured to herself, "you've read this a hundred times."

"Make it a hundred and one. You've got this," Khan encouraged, his deep, resonant voice cutting through her self-doubt. He nudged against her side, his shimmering black fur brushing her arm in a gesture that was grounding and familiar.

Jessie sucked in a breath, her gaze darting between the arcane symbols on the page and the unnerving red waters before her. She had faced down spectral hauntings and poltergeist pranks with less trepidation than this. Yet, the urgency of the river's transformation demanded more than just her usual bravery—it demanded precision.

"Okay," she said, steadying her voice as if trying to convince the very elements to align with her intent. "Here goes nothing—or everything."

Khan's tail twitched in silent applause, his eyes pooling with otherworldly light as he watched her closely. His confidence in her was an unspoken spell of its own, weaving strength into her resolve.

Jessie raised her arms, commanding the attention of the unseen forces that thrummed through the murky fog. She recited the incantation, her voice clear and unwavering, each syllable a note in the symphony of ancient magic they were invoking.

"Anubis, guide of lost souls, hear my plea..."

As her chant rose above the lap of water against the dock, Khan sat back on his haunches, his own murmurs harmonising with Jessie's voice. The air seemed to shimmer, the atmosphere charged with anticipation.

"Let the waters run pure as the sacred Nile," Jessie continued, her eyes fixed on the blood-red tide.

Bit by bit, the crimson began to fade, the murky red diluting into a clearer hue. It was as though an artist had taken an eraser to a garish painting, restoring it to a canvas of natural beauty. The magical energy emanating from Khan pulsed in rhythm with Jessie's heartbeats, amplifying the potency of her words.

"By the power of Ma'at, balance be restored!"

With the final proclamation, Jessie's arms dropped to her sides, her chest heaving with the effort of the ritual. The river, now flowing in its rightful colour, whispered its thanks in the gentle lapping of water against the stone.

"Did it work?" Jessie asked, almost afraid to believe.

"Look for yourself," Khan replied, his tone tinged with pride.

She turned to the river, her breath catching at the sight of the Mersey's waters, once again a familiar, comforting shade of greyish brown. Relief washed over her, leaving her knees weak and her spirit soaring.

"Thank you, Khan," Jessie said, her smile reflecting the dawn of triumph on her face.

"Anytime, Harper," Khan responded with a flick of his ear, his eyes still aglow—not just with magical residue, but with affection for the human who had become his closest ally in a world far from his ancient Egyptian sands.

As Jessie's pulse steadied and the last whispers of magical energy dissipated into the early morning air, Khan's ears twitched sharply. His body tensed, a ripple of unease cutting through the victory-laden silence.

"Jessie," his voice cut into her daydream, "we've got company."

Jessie looked up from her notebook, the pages still fluttering in the aftermath of their incantation. She followed Khan's gaze toward the looming shadow of Liverpool Cathedral, an ancient sentinel against the pale sky. The air felt charged, laden with a tension that was new, yet disturbingly familiar.

"Something's wrong," she murmured, feeling a cold prickle run down her spine. "The balance..."

"Disturbed, yes." Khan's green eyes narrowed, and he leapt down from his perch on the old stone wall. "A rival deity is making its move. We need to get to the cathedral—now."

"Can't we catch our breath first?" Jessie quipped, even as she scooped him up and started towards the magnificent sandstone edifice, her boots pounding against the cobbles.

"Would you rather chat or save the world?" Khan retorted, his snarkiness barely masking the urgency in his tone.

Jessie's hair whipped around her face as they hurried through the serpentine streets, the fog, now returned, swirling around them like a living entity. She knew the way by heart, but today it felt like traversing through another dimension, where every step could unleash unknown dangers.

"Khan, are you sure—" she began, but her words were swept away as they reached the foot of the cathedral.

"Trust me," Khan said, his voice a low growl as they bounded up the steps. "We don't have much time."

They moved through the shadows of the vast nave, the echoes of their footsteps blending with a faint, otherworldly hum. Reaching the spiral staircase, Jessie couldn't help but feel a sense of *déjà vu*. They had been here before, for different reasons, under different skies.

"Up we go," Khan announced, launching himself onto the first step with graceful agility.

Jessie followed, her hand tracing the cool, worn stone as they ascended higher and higher. The wind began to whistle through the gaps in the tower, a forlorn soundtrack to their daunting climb.

"Almost there," Khan encouraged, as they stepped onto the rooftop. The city stretched out below them, a tapestry of history and nineteen-thirties modernity interwoven and hidden under the blanket of fog.

"Showtime," Jessie muttered, squaring her shoulders.

In response to the challenge ahead, Khan's form shimmered, the air around him warping as ancient magic took over his very being. Before Jessie's eyes, he grew in size and stature, his sleek black fur giving way to a radiant golden mane. His true form was a sight to behold, a majestic creature of legend, power rolling off him in waves.

"By Bastet," Jessie whispered, her eyes wide with awe and not a little pride. "You never cease to amaze me, Khan."

"Save the compliments for after the battle, Harper," Khan replied, though his tone was tinged with appreciation.

"Always so modest," Jessie teased, drawing a small circle in the air with her finger, ready to channel her own brand of magic.

Together, they faced the horizon, watching as the first tendrils of malevolent energy began to seep into the waking world. Jessie's heart thrummed with alarm; whatever came next, they would face it as they always did—side by side.

The rooftop of the Liverpool Cathedral became the ancient battleground as Khan, in his resplendent form, squared off against the rival deity whose presence thickened the air with a real threat. The city below held its breath, a silent audience to a spectacle it could scarcely understand.

"Ready, Khan?" Jessie called out, her voice tinged with apprehension and a thoughtful determination that had seen them through countless scrapes.

"Born ready," came the feline's snarky retort, though his eyes were alight with an intensity born of millennia.

Jessie raised her hands, fingers weaving intricate patterns as she chanted, her voice a melodic counterpoint to the staccato bursts of energy that erupted around them. Protective barriers shimmered into existence, warding off the malevolent forces that clawed at the edges of reality.

As spells clashed overhead, brilliant and terrifying, Khan's voice boomed across the expanse, chanting incantations much older than the cathedral stones beneath their feet ... and older than the stones of Stonehenge. The rival deity, a swirl of shadows and malice, answered with howls that threatened to tear the very fabric of the world.

"Khan, left flank!" Jessie warned, her eyes never leaving the fray as she spotted a creeping tendril of darkness slithering towards them from the periphery.

"Nice try!" Khan bellowed, his tail flicking as he countered the attack with a surge of golden light that sent ripples through the fog.

The duel escalated, each exchange more furious than the last, the air alive with the scent of ozone and the crackle of raw power. Jessie's chants grew louder, more insistent; her words a beacon of hope amidst the chaos.

Then, in a moment that seemed suspended in time, Khan gathered every thread of his ancient strength, his fur standing on end, his muscles coiled like springs. With a roar that shook the heavens, he released a burst of radiant energy so pure, so focused, that it pierced through the darkness like a spear of dawn.

"Be gone!" he thundered, and the rival deity shrieked—a sound of defeat—as it dissolved, banished back to its own realm.

Silence fell like soft rain upon the aftermath. Residual wizardry hung in the air, a testament to the battle waged. Jessie slumped ever so slightly, her breaths coming in heavy sighs as relief washed over her. A profound sense of accomplishment mingled with bone-deep exhaustion, but her smile was undeniable.

"Show-off," she teased, leaning against a fearsome-looking gargoyle, her gaze softening as she took in the sight of Khan, his energy spent yet victorious.

"Couldn't have done it without you, Harper," Khan admitted, his majestic form beginning to shrink back to the sleek black cat she knew so well.

"Let's not make a habit out of this, okay? My librarian heart can't take it," Jessie quipped, the warmth in her tone wrapping around them like a comforting blanket.

"Agreed. Next time we stick to overdue books and misplaced spectres," Khan replied, already thinking of his favourite spot on the office windowsill.

Together, they stood for a moment longer, savouring the quiet triumph before turning to descend from the heights, the dawn's early light just beginning to chase away the remnants of the night's terrors.

The descent from the cathedral's rooftop was less a victory march and more a careful navigation through a maze of ancient stones and modern consequences. Jessie felt every loose pebble under her feet, heard the whisper of the waking city below, and could almost taste the tang of spent magic in the air.

"Careful there," she murmured as she stumbled slightly. Khan's once-majestic form was now small and vulnerable on her shoulder. His fur felt damp against her neck, a mixture of dew and sweat from exertion.

"You wouldn't dream of tripping up, not after all that, would you?" Khan replied, his voice lacking its usual sharp edge. It held instead a note of gratitude, an emotion he wore as comfortably as a cat donning a sweater.

Jessie couldn't help but chuckle at the image, even as her mind raced with worry. She thought they were exposed now, their secret antics no longer hidden by the veil of ignorance. The people of Liverpool had seen too much, their eyes wide with wonder and fear as the sky lit up with otherworldly power.

"Think they'll build us a statue?" Khan joked weakly, trying to lighten the mood that had settled over them like the heavy fog from earlier.

"Only if it includes a perch for you," Jessie shot back, her smile bittersweet. She knew the implications of tonight's spectacle ran deeper than heroic tales and folklore. There would be questions, fears, and perhaps even danger.

Her heart twisted at the thought of any harm coming to Khan or the city she'd come to love. Responsibility pressed down on her shoulders, heavier than the fatigued feline who already claimed residence there. She wondered if this was how Atlas felt, holding up the world, afraid to so much as shrug.

"Hey, Harper," Khan said, his voice cutting into her spiralling thoughts. "You're doing that thing again where you think too hard. It's over, we won."

"Did we?" Jessie asked, her eyes scanning the horizon where the first light of dawn was painting the sky in strokes of pink and orange. "Or did we just invite a whole new set of problems?"

"Problems, shmroblems," Khan mumbled, his head bumping gently against her cheek in an affectionate nudge. "We'll handle it. We always do."

"Spoken like a true enigmatic feline," Jessie replied with a soft sigh, feeling the warmth from his body spread through her, offering comfort amidst the chaos.

As they reached the bottom of the stone steps, the sun rose higher, casting long shadows behind them. The fog had gone. The city stirred, life resuming its rhythm, unaware of how close it had come to a different kind of awakening.

"Home then?" Khan suggested, his eyes meeting hers with a silent plea for rest.

"Home," Jessie agreed.

THE FOG THAT HAD shrouded the city in a ghostly veil had relented, revealing the worn tramlines of Dale Street and the familiar silhouette of their modest office nestled down an alley just off Dale Street. Jessie Harper turned the key in the lock, her movements deliberate, shoulders set with the weight of the night's events yet eased by the comfort of routine.

"Looks like the world's decided to give us a break with the weather, at least," she murmured, pushing open the door. The jingle of the small brass bell above it sounded like a welcome from an old friend.

"Break? Ha!" Khan's voice was huskier than usual, the toll of the magical battle not quite worn off. "We've probably got about five minutes before the next calamity hits."

Jessie chuckled, stepping into the office that doubled as their sanctuary and base of operations. She flicked on the lights, casting a warm glow over the haphazard stacks of books and the large, slightly tattered map of Liverpool pinned to one wall.

"Optimistic as ever, I see," she said, helping Khan down to his favourite cushion atop the filing cabinet. His fur seemed to shimmer even in the artificial light, the last remnants of his true form slipping away as he settled back into his comfortably compact, if no less majestic, housecat shape.

"Realistic," he corrected with a weary purr. "But if you insist on optimism, then yes, let's enjoy the calm while we can."

Jessie hung her coat on the stand by the door and took a deep breath, the scent of old paper and a hint of lavender from a sachet Khan insisted on keeping – for ambiance, he claimed – filling her nostrils. She walked to the window, watching as the early morning's sun bathed the street in a soft, golden light.

"Today's going to be a new day," she declared, more to herself than to Khan. Her hazel eyes tracked the movement of an early bird darting across the sky. "Quite literally, I suppose."

"Every day's a new day. That's how time works, Harper." Despite his snarkiness, there was a note of affection in Khan's voice that made Jessie's lips twitch into a smile.

"True," she conceded, pulling out her chair and settling behind the desk cluttered with notes and odd trinkets they'd collected on their various supernatural escapades. "But today feels different. Like we turned a page. And this next chapter... well, it might just be our toughest yet."

"Can't wait," Khan said, summoning enough energy to lift his head and lock eyes with her. "We've got ancient Egyptian magic, a librarian's resourcefulness, and a cat's nine lives on our side. Not too shabby, eh?"

"Nine lives and the curiosity to match," Jessie teased, her pen already dancing across her journal ready to document the night's events while they were fresh in her mind. "But you're right. We've handled worse. Together."

"Exactly." Khan yawned, a pink tongue curling briefly before he closed his mouth. "Now, if you don't mind, I'm going to take advantage of the rare peace and quiet. Wake me when the apocalypse is back on schedule."

"Will do," Jessie promised, her heart swelling with gratitude for her partner in all things paranormal. She glanced outside once more, noting the clear sky and the promise it held. The fog may have lifted, but their journey was far from over.

Chapter Seven

THE VEIL MENDED

JESSIE HARPER PUSHED OPEN the door to the Dale Street Private Investigations Agency, a gentle creak whispering secrets of its own as it swung inward. She stepped inside, her eyes scanning the room for any changes since they'd been away, but everything was just as they'd left it. With a soft sigh, she set her well-worn leather bag down on the desk, the surface cluttered with the bric-a-brac of their peculiar trade.

"Home sweet mystical home," she murmured, a half-smile playing at the edge of her lips.

From the corner of her eye, she watched Khan— the real brains behind their operation—leap onto the windowsill with the grace of a creature who knew more than he ever let on. His green eyes, glowing like emeralds catching the last slanting rays of daylight, swept across the room as if he could perceive things beyond the reach of mere mortals.

"Everything looks in order, I suppose," Jessie said, though the comment was more for herself than for Khan. "No goblins have turned our files into confetti, then?"

"Disappointingly mundane," came Khan's snarky reply, his voice rich with layered meaning. "But we can't all be chaos incarnate."

Jessie chuckled at that, shaking her head as she moved towards the filing cabinet. The old metal monster groaned as she pulled open the top drawer, revealing a motley collection of case files that seemed to swell with untold stories. Her fingers, gentle yet certain, brushed against the frayed edges of the folders—each one a testament to the strange and the supernatural, and her new life far removed from the quiet order of library shelves.

"Let's see what wonders await us today," Jessie said, thumbing through the files with an air of anticipation. "Ah, the case of the vanishing vicar, or perhaps the mysterious lights over the Mersey?"

"Choose wisely," Khan quipped from his sunlit perch. "Our evening plans hinge on your selection."

With a deep breath, Jessie allowed the familiar comfort of the office to envelop her. It was here, amidst the dusty tomes and arcane trinkets, that she felt most alive. Each case was a puzzle begging to be solved, and with Khan by her side, she knew there was no mystery they couldn't unravel. Together, they were a force to be reckoned with, and Liverpool's shadowy corners had learned to whisper their names with a mix of fear and respect.

"Alright, my feline oracle," Jessie said, pulling out a particularly thick file labelled 'Whispering Willows: A Haunting.' "This one should keep us busy till the kettle boils."

"Excellent choice," purred Khan, his contentment clear even as he lounged on the windowsill. "The game is afoot, as they say."

As Jessie settled into her chair, a sense of direction in her life filled her—a librarian turned sleuth, she now catalogued the uncanny, shelved the spectral, and indexed the inexplicable. And with each case, she wove another thread into the rich tapestry of their shared history, a history that was anything but ordinary.

Jessie's fingers danced over the typewriter keys, each click a meticulous step in the delicate ballet of altering records. With the precision of a seasoned librarian, she crafted plausible explanations for incidents that defied all reason—hauntings explained away as elaborate pranks, spectral apparitions reduced to tricks of the light.

"Make sure you mention the swamp gas," Khan murmured from his windowsill throne, his voice a velvet caress against the quiet hum of the office. "Humans will believe anything if you blame it on swamp gas."

Jessie chuckled softly, her hazel eyes twinkling with amusement. "Of course. Because Liverpool is teeming with swamps," she teased, her tone laced with gentle sarcasm. She could always count on Khan's snarky wisdom to lighten the mood, even when the task at hand was steeped in shadows.

"Exactly," Khan replied, his green eyes glinting with mischief. "It's all about the delivery, Jessie. Now, onto the next order of business."

With a graceful leap that belied his fatigue, Khan landed beside Jessie, his black fur shimmering subtly in the afternoon light. He nudged a small vial toward her—a concoction of herbs and oils only they knew the true power of.

"Remember, just three drops," he instructed, his voice a low purr that seemed to resonate through the very walls of the office. "And focus on the intent. The memories need to be softened, not shattered."

Jessie nodded, her hands steady as she uncorked the vial. She measured out the drops with care, each one falling into the ritual circle they had drawn earlier. As she worked, Khan's presence by her side was as comforting as a well-worn book—a reminder that no matter how strange life became, she wasn't facing it alone.

"Concentrate, Jessie," Khan whispered, his eyes half-closed as he guided her through the incantation. "Envision the memories like pages in a book, turning back, becoming unreadable."

Closing her eyes, Jessie did as instructed. She pictured the words of yesterday's chaos becoming blurred, the edges of recollection curling and fading like ancient parchment. Her heart beat in time with the silent rhythm of the spell, and she felt a kinship with the magic—a sense of belonging that had nothing to do with the world of card catalogues and late fees.

"Perfect," Khan said, his tone soft but proud. "You're a natural."

Opening her eyes, Jessie saw the faintest glow dissipate from the circle, the air settling back into a normal state. She let out a breath she hadn't realised she'd been holding, a smile tugging at the corners of her mouth. It was a small victory, perhaps, but one that brought a sense of peace to the Dale Street Private Investigations Agency office—a haven for the unexplained in a city that never truly slept.

Jessie's fingers hovered momentarily above the final symbol etched into the desk's surface, the lines drawn in salt and infused with her intent. Khan sat beside her, his emerald gaze fixed upon the pattern, tail flicking with anticipation. "Now," he said, his voice a velvety command that seemed to resonate with the charged atmosphere of the room.

With a decisive motion, Jessie swept her hand through the symbol, scattering the salt. The air hummed, vibrated, then settled. She watched, awestruck, as the ambient energy pulsed once—a luminous heartbeat—and faded into nothingness.

"Did it work?" she asked, the question wrapped in hope.

Khan's whiskers twitched with amusement. "You doubt your own prowess? Take a look."

Jessie leaned back in her chair, an involuntary smile breaking across her face as she recognised the true magnitude of her accomplishment. They had done it; the magic had woven seamlessly through reality, altering just enough to keep the world oblivious to the wonders and dangers they so often subdued.

"Tea?" she offered, still riding the high of success.

"Only if you've perfected that peculiar human art of brewing or mashing as you call it," Khan teased, his snarky affection warming the room further.

Before Jessie could respond, a gentle breeze fluttered through the open window, carrying with it the sounds of Liverpool stirring from its enchantment-induced slumber. The fog outside was still absent, revealing the paved streets and the grand limestone facades of the neighbouring buildings. Pedestrians resumed their hurried walks: men wearing dapper suits and hats, the ladies wearing the latest fashions and cloche hats. Their voices a distant murmur, interwoven with the rhythmic clatter of horse-drawn carriages, the sounds of the combustion engine rolling by, and the rattle of trams and the overhead railway affectionately known as the 'Dockers Umbrella.'

"Ah, the symphony of the everyday," Khan mused, his eyes half-closed as he savoured the return to the *status quo*. "It has its charm, doesn't it?"

"Charm and chaos," Jessie agreed, standing to stretch her legs. She approached the window and rested her arms on the sill, watching as the city reclaimed its rhythm. It was a dance she knew well, one that echoed the steady beat of her heart—an affirmation of life continuing, regardless of the secrets hidden just beneath its surface.

"Come on," she said, turning back toward Khan with a playful glint in her eyes. "Let's get that tea before we're out solving the next mystery that this city throws our way."

Khan leapt off the windowsill with a grace that belied his weariness. "Lead the way, dear Jessie. After all, who am I to deny the simple pleasures of a well-earned cuppa?"

JESSIE UNFOLDED HERSELF FROM the chair, her limbs grateful for the reprieve. She arched her back with a soft sigh, feeling the pleasant pull of muscles waking from their static slumber. As she did so, her gaze roamed lovingly over the Dale Street Private Investigations Agency office—a place that had become both a haven and a headquarters. The walls, once strangers, now knew of tales of the cases they'd seen resolved under this very roof.

"Quite the journey from Dewey Decimals to mystical dilemmas, eh?" Jessie mused aloud, her voice tinged with the warmth of reminiscence. Khan simply blinked in response, his tail flicking as if to punctuate her sentiment.

Turning her attention back to the task at hand, Jessie approached her desk with a fresh mind after her nap. She began sifting through the case files with the methodical precision of a maestro composing a symphony. Each folder was an instrument, each report a note to be harmonised into the greater melody of their work.

"Let's see," she murmured, neatly aligning the folders into stacks. "Ghosts go here, poltergeists there... Ah, and the doppelgänger debacle deserves its own color-coded tab."

Her fingers, adept from years of navigating card catalogues and arranging bookshelves, danced over the files. She crafted labels with careful calligraphy, a librarian's touch transforming the mundane task into an art form. Every file was meticulously annotated, bridging the divide between the normal and the not-so-much.

"Order from chaos, Khan. Isn't that what we do best?" Jessie quipped, glancing over her shoulder at her feline companion. Khan regarded her with an expression that could only be described as politely amused—or at least as much as a cat's features would allow.

"Indeed, Jessie. Though I must say, your penchant for organisation is nothing short of magical itself," Khan replied, his tone rich with the rumble of a satisfied purr.

She chuckled, tucking a stray auburn lock behind her ear. "Well, when you're dealing with enchanted objects and wayward spirits, a little paperwork magic goes a long way."

Together, Jessie and Khan surveyed the newly ordered realm of their agency. Each file, a chronicle of adventures past, stood ready to aid them in unravelling the mysteries yet to come. With every detail in its proper place, Jessie felt a sense of serenity settle upon the room—like the last piece of a puzzle snugly fitting into the grand picture of their lives.

The brass hands of the antique clock perched on the mantlepiece nudged ever closer to the hour, a silent herald that the day was waning. Noting the time with a nod, Jessie pushed back from her desk and rose, her limbs grateful for the stretch after hours spent in meticulous organisation.

"Tea time again, Khan," she announced, as if the ritual needed any introduction between the two. The kettle, a stout little thing with more dents than a shield in a knight's armoury, found its way onto the kitchenette stove with a familiar clink.

Khan shifted his position on the windowsill, a throne befitting an ancient Egyptian deity turned detective's side-kick. His green eyes trailed Jessie's movements, the afternoon sun casting glimmers across his sleek black fur.

"Earl Grey or chamomile today?" Jessie asked, peering over her shoulder, a playful quirk to her brow. It was a needless question; their preferences had long since become routine, but the small talk added a comforting layer to the sacred tea-making ceremony.

"Earl Grey, I believe," Khan's voice held the smooth confidence of one who knew the answer before the question was posed. "We could use the robust flavour after today's endeavours. But mine must be served cold."

"Robust and cold it is," Jessie chuckled, measuring out the leaves with a precision that spoke of a ritual often repeated, yet always savoured. Water bubbled and hissed as it transformed from liquid to steam, a tiny tempest contained within the kettle.

She poured the scalding water over the leaves in the tea pot and the room filled with the rich scent of bergamot.

The aroma weaved through the air, wrapping around the pair like a warm embrace. Jessie set the steeping brew aside and fetched the cups—two mismatched pieces of porcelain that seemed to have found each other by some twist of fate, much like herself and Khan.

"Your cup awaits, Your Highness, just wait until it gets cold," she teased, placing the steaming vessel beside Khan, careful not to disturb his comfortable repose.

"Ah, your generosity knows no bounds," Khan replied, his tone laced with affectionate sarcasm as he glanced down at the offering. Yet, the look he cast Jessie was nothing short of fondness, an acknowledgment of the simple comforts they shared in their corner of the world.

Jessie leaned against the edge of the desk, cradling her own cup, feeling the warmth seep into her palms. She watched Khan for a moment, the cat now languidly stretching before settling back into his cushioned spot.

"Days like these make me appreciate the quiet moments," she mused aloud, her eyes reflecting the glow of satisfaction that comes from a job well done.

"Quiet moments and good company," Khan agreed, his voice a soft rumble as he settled in to watch the city go about its business.

They sat there in companionable silence, the office a bastion of tranquillity in the midst of Liverpool's daily bustle. Outside, life carried on, the ordinary and the extraordinary intertwined, much like the files Jessie had so carefully sorted—a testament to the partnership that thrived within these four walls, where the line between normal and paranormal blurred into insignificance.

Jessie settled back into the creaking embrace of her well-worn office chair, a steaming cup of tea cradled between her hands. The delicate scent of Earl Grey tea mingled with the dusty tang of old paper and magic that always seemed to linger in the air of Dale Street Private Investigations Agency. She breathed in deeply, letting the herbal fragrance soothe her senses and calm her mind.

"Nothing quite like it, is there?" she whispered to herself, a small smile playing on her lips.

Khan, from his sun-dappled perch on the windowsill, offered a low purr in response, his eyes mere slits of emerald contentment. "Indeed," he intoned lazily, without opening his eyes. "The perfect brew after a day's toil... as long as it's cold."

Jessie chuckled softly at his melodramatic tone and took a tentative sip, feeling the warmth spread through her. Her gaze softened as she watched Khan, his sleek black fur absorbing the golden light that streamed through the window and wondered how anyone could drink Earl Grey cold.

"Remember when my biggest concern was late book returns?" Jessie mused out loud, her mind wandering back to the days when her life revolved around the hushed corridors of the library.

"Ah, but those dusty tomes were your training ground," Khan replied, finally cracking open one eye to regard her with a playful glint. "Each spine you shelved, every index card you filed... all preparation for the mysteries we unravel now."

Jessie laughed, the sound echoing gently off the high ceilings. "I suppose Dewey Decimal never anticipated his system would be used to categorise poltergeists and potion mishaps."

"Life," Khan said, sitting up to stretch leisurely, "is an ever-evolving catalogue, my dear. You've simply embraced a new genre."

"True enough," Jessie agreed, setting down her tea cup and pausing to admire the neat rows of files on her desk. Each label represented a case, a story, a secret; some mundane, others steeped in enchantments only they could see. Her fingers traced the edge of a folder labelled 'The Case of the Vanishing Ventriloquist,' a hint of pride flickering in her eyes.

"From librarian to keeper of the supernatural," she reflected, "not the career path I envisioned, but certainly more... exhilarating."

"Exhilarating, indeed," Khan agreed, amusement lacing his voice. "And who better to chronicle our adventures than someone who once safeguarded human knowledge?"

"Quite the pair we make," Jessie replied warmly, her eyes meeting Khan's in a silent exchange of understanding and mutual respect. They were partners, co-authors in a series of tales that straddled the line between the seen and unseen, the known and the mysterious.

"Here's to many more chapters," Khan purred, raising an imaginary glass.

"Many more," Jessie affirmed, picking up her tea once again, a soft smile curving her lips. Together, they faced the unknown, each challenge another page in their shared narrative, ready to be written with care, curiosity, and a dash of librarian's precision.

The hours passed and the sun dipped lower in the sky, its waning light casting long shadows across the Dale Street Private Investigations Agency office. As the glow softened to a golden hue, Jessie savoured the stillness that enveloped the space, feeling the energy of Liverpool's streets fade into a muted hum behind the glass pane. Khan, perched on the windowsill, watched the day surrender to dusk, his eyes reflecting the tranquillity of the hour.

"Another day navigated," Jessie mused aloud, her voice a whisper in the settled quiet.

"Charted and plotted like a map of the stars," Khan replied sagely, his tail curling around him in contentment.

Jessie chuckled at his grandiose analogy, glancing over her shoulder at him. "Do you suppose we'll ever run out of mysteries?" she asked, half-joking, half-wistful.

"Only when the stars cease to shine," Khan quipped back, and they lapsed into a companionable silence, each lost in their reflections.

With a gentle sigh, Jessie rose from her chair, stretching languidly. She began tidying the desk with measured care, her fingers lingering on each file as she organised them into neat piles. The heavy cardstock whispered under her touch, a rustling chorus accompanying the dance of her hands. Every file held stories of otherworldly adventures and unexplained phenomena—each one a chapter in the book of their lives.

"Remember this one?" Jessie pulled out a particularly thick folder, the edges more frayed than the others.

Khan's ears perked up, and he glanced over with a knowing look. "How could I forget? The Poltergeist Pantomime. A performance worthy of an encore."

She laughed softly, placing the file into the cabinet with reverence. It slotted in beside the others, a new addition to their archive of the arcane. Every case was meticulously documented, thanks to Jessie's librarian roots—a blend of methodical organisation and a touch of the mystical.

"Perhaps we should start a library of our own," she suggested, tapping the metal cabinet fondly. "Shelves filled with tales of the inexplicable."

"A library where every book reveals secrets," Khan mused, picturing the collection in his mind's eye.

"Whispers or yowls secrets, depending on the case," Jessie added with a wink, giving a final pat to the stack of files before closing the cabinet door with a soft click.

"Yowls are more your style, my feline friend," she teased, earning a chuff of amusement from Khan. They shared a smile, their partnership a harmonious blend of wit and wisdom.

"Indeed," Khan said, his tone brimming with faux indignation. "I do have a reputation to uphold."

As Jessie straightened the last of the papers, the room felt like an extension of themselves—every object a testament to their journey, from the mystical artefacts lining the shelves to the ancient Egyptian statuette that seemed to wink at them from atop the bookcase. Their office was more than just four walls; it was the heart of their curious existence.

"Home sweet mystical home," Jessie declared, satisfaction colouring her words.

"Until the next mystery beckons," Khan agreed, his gaze drifting back to the window and the world beyond.

And in that moment, as the afternoon light finally surrendered to evening, Jessie and Khan revelled in the peace of their sanctuary, a duo against the darkness, their bond unspoken but deeply felt.

Jessie slung her well-worn satchel over her shoulder and gave the office one last glance. Khan, with the agility that belied his ancient soul, leapt from the window ledge to join her at the door. "Ready for a bit of fresh air?" she asked, though it was more of a statement than a question.

"Always," Khan replied, his voice holding the soft rumble of distant thunder. "The evening holds secrets just waiting to be nudged into the light."

The door creaked softly as Jessie pulled it open, a sound that seemed to resonate with the closing of another successful chapter in their unconventional chronicles. She stepped over the threshold, her boots clicking against the wood floor, then the stairs and street outside as Khan followed, his feline form slipping through the opening with silent grace.

The air outside was cool, carrying the scent of rain yet to fall and the salt tang of the nearby Mersey River. Mist curled around streetlamps like dancers in slow motion, casting an ethereal glow on the buildings of Liverpool. Jessie inhaled deeply, letting the familiar smells ground her after hours spent amidst ancient texts and arcane enchantments.

"Ah, the misty caress of our dear city," Khan observed, looking up at the sky where only the faintest outlines of stars could be glimpsed. "It's like being wrapped in a cosy, albeit damp, blanket."

"Could do with less damp sometimes," Jessie chuckled, tucking a stray auburn curl behind her ear. Her hazel eyes sparkled with mirth as she caught the twinkle of amusement in Khan's green gaze.

They began to walk, their steps synchronised, a testament to the countless adventures they had shared. Each footfall seemed to echo with the whispered promises of riddles yet unsolved and spirits whose stories were half-told.

"Think we'll ever have a night without the promise of mystery?" Jessie mused aloud, watching as a horse-drawn goods cart clattered past, its lanterns swaying gently.

"Darling Jessie," Khan said, the corner of his mouth twitching upward in a smile that wasn't quite a smile, "for us, mystery is as certain as the turning of the pages in one of your beloved books."

"Then let's hope the next page brings something thrilling," she said, her wit as sharp as the edge of a librarian's bookmark.

"Or at least something that doesn't involve cleaning ectoplasm from my fur," Khan quipped, prompting a laugh from Jessie that danced in the air like music.

Their laughter mingled with the evening sounds of the city, a melody of life and the unseen magic that pulsed beneath its surface. And as they disappeared into the misty veil, it was clear that Jessie and Khan were more than mere inhabitants of Liverpool—they were guardians of its hidden wonders, shepherds of its ghostly tales, ready to face whatever the world may hold.

Chapter Eight

GUARDIANS OF THE VEIL

IN THE COSY CONFINES of the Dale Street Private Investigations Agency, Jessie Harper sorted through the pile of notes scattered across her desk—a constellation of clues that might as well have been a map to the stars for all the sense they made. She adjusted her glasses and leaned over them with the kind of focus she used to reserve for ancient texts back in her library days.

"Another missing person, Khan," Jessie murmured, her voice tinged with determination. "That's the third this month, all vanishing in the Mersey Tunnel."

From his vantage point on the desk, Khan, the enigmatic feline with fur as black as midnight and eyes like emerald orbs, watched her with an almost human curiosity. His tail flicked, writing invisible letters in the air, while the rest of him remained still as the Sphinx whose lineage he shared.

"Curiouser and curiouser," Khan purred, his tone dripping with intrigue. "The spirits are restless in the underbelly of Liverpool, or so it seems. By the way, you do know the tunnel's official name is Queensway and it is over two miles long?"

"I do," Jessie said, "how could I forget. I was there at the opening ceremony last year when King George V did the honours in front of two-hundred-thousand people. The *Daily Post* called it the "eighth wonder of the world."

"So, I'm the ninth?" Khan said.

Jessie couldn't help but smile at Khan's theatrics, a reminder of how far she'd come from shushing patrons and organising bookshelves. She stood up, stretching her back and feeling the familiar thrill of a new case tickle her spine.

"I must admit, I'm excited, Khan. But there's also this knot in my stomach," Jessie confessed, tucking a loose strand of auburn hair behind her ear. "It's one thing to read about mysteries in books; it's another to face them head-on."

Khan languidly uncurled himself from his lounging position and hopped down with the grace of a creature not bound by the laws of mere mortals. He sauntered over to her side, his eyes glinting with mischief.

"Ah, but you forget, dear Jessie," Khan said, his snarky tone belied by the affectionate nudge of his head against her leg. "You are not alone in this dance with the unknown. Plus, you've got more courage in your little finger than most have in their entire being. And let's not overlook my vast knowledge and charm."

"Charm, indeed," Jessie chuckled, bending down to scratch Khan behind his ears. The warmth of their connection shimmered in the air, an ever-present silent testament to their bond.

"Come on then, let's unravel this mystery." Jessie's eyes sparkled with anticipation. "After all, who better than us to shine a light in dark places?"

"Lead the way, intrepid investigator," Khan replied with a hint of pride. "I'll watch our backs."

Together, they stepped away from the cluttered desk and towards the door, ready to explore the depths of the Mersey Tunnel and whatever secrets it held.

Jessie snapped her case shut, the sound echoing through the office like the final note of a symphony. It was laden with tools of her newfound trade—a silver compass that quivered towards the supernatural, a vial of salt from the Dead Sea, and various other oddities only a seasoned investigator of the paranormal would carry. Beside these lay an ancient tome of spells, its leather cover worn to a soft sheen by the passage of time—and frequent consultations.

"Ready, Khan?" she asked, slipping the strap of the case over her shoulder. The weight of it was both a comfort and a reminder of the seriousness of their venture.

"Always," came the feline's reply, his tone brimming with the sort of anticipation one might have before a grand feast—or in his case, a tantalising mystery. He leapt off the desk, landing on all fours with nary a whisper of sound.

They exited the office to find the fog had returned. Jessie locked the door behind them. The streets of Liverpool greeted them with a swirling waltz of fog, thick as cream and just as enveloping. Jessie's breath misted before her, each exhalation a ghostly apparition joining the dance. Khan, ever unperturbed by the elements, trotted beside her, his black fur barely distinguishable from the blurred shadows that clung to the paving stones.

"Feels like the city is holding its breath, doesn't it?" Jessie mused, her words muffled by the dense air.

"Or it's waiting for something to breathe life into it," Khan remarked, his voice a silken purr of intrigue. "Perhaps that's our cue."

Streetlamps loomed like sentinels, their orbs reduced to dim halos that fought a losing battle against the encroaching murk. The usual cacophony of Liverpool's nightlife was hushed, sounds smothered under the heavy blanket of fog. Footsteps echoed, distorted and distant, while the foghorns repeated their strident warnings to shipping on the River Mersey.

"Even the lampposts look like they're shivering," Jessie said with a small laugh, pulling her coat tighter around her.

"Let's hope that's not an omen," Khan quipped, though his steady gaze scanned their surroundings with the astuteness of a guardian spirit. "After all, omens are notoriously unreliable narrators."

"Good thing I have you to interpret them, then." Jessie smiled down at him, appreciative of his company and the uncanny sense that with Khan by her side, even the unseen had nowhere to hide.

They continued their trek, the fog parting reluctantly before Jessie's determined stride and the silent command of Khan's presence. The Queensway tunnel awaited, its own brand of darkness a challenge they were more than ready to meet.

Jessie's boots clacked against the damp pavements and cobblestones, their rhythm steady as she and Khan neared the tunnel. The air hung thick with mist, a blanket of anticipation that seemed to shroud the grand entrance. She paused, her gaze lifting to the yawning mouth of the tunnel—a silent behemoth waiting to swallow them whole.

"Quite the gullet on this one, eh?" Khan mused from beside her, his tone light yet laden with an undercurrent of excitement. "I'd wager it's seen things more indigestible than us."

Jessie chuckled, the sound bouncing oddly against the stone facade. "I suppose we're just a snack in comparison." But there was a tremor of trepidation beneath her humour, a librarian's caution against the unknown pages of history.

"Considering our track record," Khan replied, the green glint in his eyes sharpening, "I'd say we're more of an acquired taste." His snarky assurance was like a talisman, warding off the unease that nipped at Jessie's resolve.

"Right you are, Khan." Jessie drew a deep breath, squaring her shoulders. "Let's not keep our mystery waiting any longer."

With purpose renewed, Jessie stepped forward, the lantern in her hand casting a warm glow that cut through the fog's embrace. They crossed the threshold, and the cool, earthy scent of the tunnel enveloped them, its walls echoing their entry with hints of secrecy.

Khan paced silently at her side, a shadow given form and grace. As they ventured deeper, the edges of the world dimmed until only the lantern's sphere of influence held sway over the darkness. And then, like distant stars piercing the night, Khan's eyes began to glow—a faint, otherworldly luminescence that lent an ethereal quality to the journey.

"Keep those lights up, Khan. I have a feeling we'll need all the sight we can get down here," Jessie said, her voice betraying none of the awe she felt at the eerie beauty of her companion's gift.

"Always at your service," Khan replied, a purr of amusement threading through his words. "And remember, it's not the darkness in the tunnel we need to worry about—it's whatever decides to hide in it."

"Then let's hope we're the scarier things lurking in these shadows," Jessie said, a wry smile playing on her lips as they pressed on, their partnership a beacon against the depths that awaited.

The echo of their footsteps, a staccato rhythm against the pedestrian gangway's paving stones, was the only sound that dared to travel with them as they delved further into the Mersey Tunnel. Jessie's breath came out in visible puffs, mingling with the musty air that seemed to have been trapped for centuries. The tiled walls glistened with condensation, and from somewhere deep within the bowels of the tunnel, the steady drip-drip-drip of water played a haunting melody.

"Feels like we're walking through a ghost's sigh," Jessie murmured, her gaze flitting over the uneven surfaces where shadows cavorted with the light of her lantern.

"Or perhaps the ghost is merely breathing on our necks, waiting for us to turn around," Khan quipped, his whiskers twitching in the dimness.

Jessie chuckled, though the laughter didn't quite reach her eyes. "Let's not give the spirits any ideas."

As they moved onward, the air grew heavier, thick with the weight of untold secrets. Jessie ran her fingers along the wall, feeling the chill seep into her skin. It was there that she noticed something peculiar—a series of faint etchings nearly hidden beneath recent layers of grime. She halted, squinting at the designs that seemed to dance before her eyes.

"Khan, look at these." She tilted the lantern, casting light upon the carvings. "Symbols. They're old, very old. Much older than the tunnel."

Khan approached, his tail swishing thoughtfully. He studied the markings with an intensity that belied his usual nonchalance. "Ah, yes," he said, his tone shifting to one of reverence. "These are no mere doodles of bored tunnel workers. They are wards, protective spells from an age when magic was as common as the rats in this tunnel when it was under construction."

"Protective?" Jessie echoed, her curiosity piqued. "From what?"

"From things that slink and creep and seek to do harm," Khan replied, his eyes narrowing as he scanned the symbols. "They're woven into the very stones, a tapestry of ancient power meant to safeguard the city above."

"Seems like they might need some reinforcing," Jessie said, half-joking. "Given our current case of disappearances."

"Indeed," Khan agreed, his gaze still locked on the symbols. "But let's not dawdle on history too long. We have our own creeping to do."

"Right," Jessie said, taking a deep breath and stepping away from the wall. "Let's press on. But maybe keep an eye out for anything that looks... particularly safeguard-y."

"Always," Khan assured her, his voice a soothing rumble. "After all, who better than an enigmatic feline to spot the arcane?"

With a shared nod, they continued their journey, wrapped in the cloak of mystery that the tunnel provided. Jessie felt a certain thrill at the prospect of uncovering its secrets, with Khan by her side and the whispers of the past echoing around them.

The soft halo of Jessie's lantern did little to fend off the oppressive darkness that enveloped them as they ventured deeper into the Queensway tunnel. With each cautious step, their shadows danced upon the damp walls, a silent ballet to the soundtrack of water droplets keeping time on the man-made construction materials.

"Khan, do you feel that?" Jessie whispered, the hair on her arms standing at attention. "Like we're not alone?"

"Considering we're in a public tunnel, that's entirely possible," Khan quipped, but his ears twitched toward the unseen depths. "Though I suspect you mean something less pedestrian."

"Pedestrian is the key. They are not allowed into the tunnel and don't you think it's strange that we haven't seen any vehicles since we entered the tunnel?" Jessie said.

Before Khan could respond, a figure emerged from the obscurity, a mere wisp of presence at first that solidified into a silhouette against the faint light. Jessie's heart skipped, and her hand darted to the leather-bound tome at her belt, fingers ready to trace the intricate runes etched on its cover.

"Who goes there?" she called, her voice steady despite the adrenaline flowing through her veins.

"Easy, stranger," Khan murmured, slipping between Jessie and the visitor. His form seemed to swell, a subtle shift reminding any who might challenge them that this was no ordinary cat.

"Sorry, didn't mean to startle you," came the reply from the shadows. The figure stepped forward, revealing himself under the dim glow of Jessie's lantern. He was a man of medium height, with an easy posture that belied his alertness. "Name's Thomas. I'm investigating the disappearances."

"Are you now?" Jessie eased, though her grip on the spell book remained firm. "What brings another sleuth to this particular scene of the spectral?"

"Let's just say my interests are... uniquely aligned with your current predicament," Thomas answered, eyeing Khan with a mixture of curiosity and respect. "I've been tracking certain... anomalies. And I have reason to believe we may be looking for the same thing."

"Anomalies," Jessie repeated, exchanging a glance with Khan. "That's one word for it."

"Indeed," Khan said, his stance relaxing slightly. "We've noticed certain... irregularities ourselves. Protective wards, old as the hills—or in this case, the river—compromised."

"Compromised wards?" Thomas looked genuinely intrigued. "That is concerning. I've got some theories, and perhaps together we might—"

"Pool our resources?" Jessie finished for him, a small smile breaking through her professional demeanour. "Seems like the wise thing to do, doesn't it, Khan?"

"Collaboration is often the key to unravelling the tangled skeins of mystery," the enigmatic feline agreed, his tail flicking with a hint of amusement. "And two heads are better than one, although in our case, I dare say it's more like one and a half."

"Hey!" Jessie feigned indignation but couldn't help the laugh that followed. "Which one of us is the half, then?"

"Darling, I would never imply anything other than your full competence," Khan purred, his eyes glinting. "But let's not forget who has nine lives here."

"Fair point," Jessie conceded, turning back to their newfound ally. "Alright, Thomas, lead the way. But let's tread carefully; the unknown has a way of surprising even the best of us."

"Agreed," Thomas nodded, and together, the trio delved further into the tunnel's mouth, where secrets waited in the shadows, eager to be discovered.

The damp air of the Mersey Tunnel clung to Jessie Harper's skin as she, Khan, and their unexpected companion, Thomas, pressed on. The trio moved with a stealth learned from untold encounters with the supernatural. Each step echoed with a soft splash, reverberating through the tunnel like whispers of the lost.

"Notice anything peculiar about the construction here?" Thomas asked, his voice hushed but clear in the close confines of the underground thoroughfare.

"Other than it being an excellent place for a haunting?" Jessie said with a wry twist to her lips, running her fingers along the cold, gritty wall. "It's older than it looks. These tiles have seen more than just the passing of cars and lorries."

"Exactly," Thomas affirmed with a nod. "I've been mapping out energy fluctuations. And they all converge towards..."

"Towards that?" Khan interjected, his eyes narrowing at a faint outline shimmering against the darkness ahead.

"Indeed," Jessie murmured, drawing closer. She saw the subtle glow emanating from a section of the wall that seemed unremarkably blank to the untrained eye. But as they approached, the wall revealed its secret: a hidden chamber, veiled by ancient enchantments now faltering under some unseen strain.

"Magical anomaly," Jessie said as she reached into her leather satchel. The tome of spells felt like an old friend under her fingertips, its worn cover crackling as she flipped through the pages.

"Seems we've found the heart of our problem," Khan remarked dryly, his whiskers twitching. "Or rather, the heart has found us."

"Can you neutralise it?" Thomas peered over Jessie's shoulder at the cryptic symbols dancing across the aged paper.

"Neutralising is what we do best," Jessie said with a confidence that had grown roots deep within her since leaving the quiet life of a librarian behind. She pointed at a spell marked with a star in the margin. "This one. It resonates with the wards outside. If we can reinforce them, we should be able to contain whatever this... thing is... or does."

"Let's get to it, then," Khan said, stepping forward. His form shimmered for a moment, hinting at the shapeshifter magic streaming through his body. "I'll provide the channelling focus. You handle the incantation."

"Right," Jessie agreed, taking a deep breath. She began to recite the words written on the page, her voice steady despite the flicker of apprehension in her chest. As she spoke, Khan's eyes glowed brighter, casting an otherworldly light over the chamber.

The air thickened, charged with power as the spell took hold. The anomaly—a swirling vortex of shadows and whispered secrets—pulsed like a living thing, fighting against the encroaching light.

"Keep going, Jessie! You're doing splendidly!" Khan encouraged, though his tone betrayed the effort it took to maintain their magical shield.

"Almost there..." Jessie's voice wavered but did not break, the final syllables of the spell ringing out with authority. With a sound like the snapping of ancient chains, the anomaly shrank, its darkness dissipating until nothing remained but the echo of its presence.

"Is it..." Thomas began, but Jessie nodded before he could finish.

"Contained," she confirmed, closing her tome with a satisfied snap. "The wards are holding. For now, at least."

"Excellent work," Khan purred, though fatigue pulled at the edges of his snarky demeanour. "I daresay we make quite the team, Jessie Harper."

"Couldn't have done it without you, Khan," Jessie replied, a warm smile lighting up her features. "Or your nine lives."

"Let's hope it doesn't come to using any of those," Khan quipped, his tail giving a lazy swish as he regained his usual composure.

"Agreed," Thomas said, a note of admiration in his tone. "You two are quite the pair. I'm glad we crossed paths tonight."

"Us too, Thomas," Jessie said as they turned back toward the Liverpool end of the tunnel. "Who knows what other mysteries await us in the shadows of Liverpool?"

"Whatever they are," Khan added with a confident flick of his ears, "we'll face them together."

Stepping away from the chamber where they had just averted disaster, Jessie dusted her hands off on her coat, the leather tome tucked safely under her arm. She glanced at Khan, whose black fur seemed to drink in the pale light of their lantern. "Not bad for a night's work?"

"Understatement of the century," Khan replied with his usual dry wit. His green eyes sparkled with a mix of pride and mischief. "You have to admit, though, we do have a certain... flair for the dramatic."

"Flair?" Jessie chuckled. "If by 'flair' you mean narrowly escaping being swallowed by a magical vortex, then yes, absolutely."

Thomas, the investigator who had stumbled into their investigation, stood nearby, shaking his head in disbelief. "I've seen some things in my time," he said, "but you two... You're something else. If you ever need an extra pair of hands, or eyes, I'd be honoured to lend them."

"Thanks, Thomas," Jessie said with genuine appreciation. "It's always good to know we've got allies out there. Liverpool can be a dark place, but it feels a bit brighter knowing we're not alone."

"Indeed," Khan agreed, offering a regal nod that somehow didn't seem out of place, even in the dank confines of the Queensway tunnel.

The trio made their way back towards the entrance, the air growing fresher with each step they took. The menacing echo of their footsteps was now just a memory, replaced by the soft sounds of their camaraderie. Jessie exhausted but it was a good kind of tired—the kind that comes after doing something worthwhile.

"Feels like we're walking towards a new dawn," Jessie mused as they neared the exit, the outlines of the tunnel mouth visible in the distance.

"Let's not get ahead of ourselves," Khan cautioned. "It's still Liverpool; dawn is more of a concept than an actual event." His comment drew a round of laughter, dispelling the last remnants of the evening's tension.

Emerging from the tunnel, they were met with the misty caress of pre-dawn fog. It swirled around them, not as an ominous cloak as it had been before, but as a soft veil, gently yielding to the promise of the morning light. Jessie took a deep breath, relishing the crisp air that seemed to herald new beginnings.

"Look at that," she said, gesturing toward the dissipating fog. "The city's waking up. And after tonight, I think we'll be seeing a lot more of what it has to hide."

"Count on it," Khan said, his tail high and confident. "With you by my side, Jessie Harper, I say bring on the hidden corners and shadowed alleys."

"Always," Jessie agreed, her voice steady and resolute. They turned their backs to the tunnel, its darkness now just another chapter in their book of paranormal mysteries. Hand in hand with history and magic, Jessie and Khan stepped forward into the hushed streets, ready for whatever secrets awaited their discovery.

The key turned with a satisfying click, and Jessie Harper pushed open the door to the Dale Street Private Investigations Agency. The familiar scent of old books and the faint tang of Earl Grey tea enveloped her like a welcoming embrace. Khan sauntered in behind her, his black fur catching the early morning light that filtered through the blinds.

"Home sweet office," Jessie murmured, setting down her bag with a soft thud. She flexed her fingers, still tingling from the residual magic of the night's work.

Khan leapt up onto his favoured spot on the windowsill, his green eyes reflecting the cityscape as he glanced out over Liverpool's awakening streets. "You did well, Jessie," he said, his voice threaded with pride. "This city doesn't know how lucky it is to have you."

Jessie chuckled, shaking her head as she began to sort through her notes. "We make a pretty great team, don't we?" she replied, glancing at Khan with affection.

"Team?" Khan feigned insult, arching an eyebrow. "I'd say I'm more of the brains of the operation." His tail flicked playfully, and Jessie laughed, knowing full well that their banter was part of the fabric of their relationship—a tapestry woven with snarkiness and sentiment in equal measure.

She pulled out the tome of spells they'd used in the tunnel, its leather cover worn but resilient. As she placed it carefully on the shelf, her gaze lingered on the spines of the other mystical volumes they had collected over time. Each one held stories and solutions to the curious cases they'd encountered.

"Alright, let's get these findings documented before my brain decides to take an unscheduled nap," Jessie declared, rolling up her sleeves as she approached the typewriter. The clack of keys punctuated the silence, a rhythmic soundtrack to their productivity.

Khan, meanwhile, began to meticulously clean his whiskers, though his attention remained on Jessie. "Just think, with each case we close, we're peeling back another layer of this city's secrets," he mused.

"Endless possibilities for adventure," Jessie agreed, her eyes alight with anticipation. "And who knows what we'll uncover next?"

"Whatever it is, we'll face it together," Khan said resolutely, jumping down to weave between Jessie's legs in a show of solidarity.

"Always together," Jessie confirmed, reaching down to stroke Khan's shimmering fur. A sense of contentment settled over them both as they looked around their cosy office, fortified by their triumphs and the unbreakable bond they shared.

With the dawn of a new day casting golden hues across the room, Jessie Harper and Khan prepared for whatever mysteries awaited them next in the city they called home.

<h1 style="text-align:center">Epilogue</h1>

Jessie had a few hours to reflect on all that happened in the Queensway tunnel before George, Isabel, and Agnes returned to their respective duties with the agency. She was staring at the window where Khan was perched in his usual spot when she gave voice to one of her thoughts.

"Khan, something bothers me about the man we met in the tunnel."

"Thomas? How so?" Khan said with a grin.

"Was he real? If so, he's another one who knows you can talk and possess magic powers. I find it odd you never mentioned this," Jessie said.

"Odd, schmodd, it's elementary my dear Jessie."

"How so?"

"First of all, allow me to congratulate you on discovering my ruse. Here is the truth. I didn't know exactly what forces we were dealing with in the tunnel so to reinforce my hand, or paw so to speak, I conjured up Thomas to make the vortex believe it was dealing with three adversaries with powers to overcome it. It worked."

"Splendid, Khan, you are clever," Jessie said.

"I fail to agree because I haven't yet mastered how to transform me into two separate forms and both talk at the same time," Khan said, "but other than that, yes, I am purrfect."

"Khan, you are incorrigible," Jessie teasingly admonished Khan who was much more than a beloved pet. "Now, let's get the car and go and pick up the gang at Lime Street station."

GEORGE'S TRAIN ARRIVED FIRST. He had been to Blackpool to visit a war time colleague. They didn't have long to wait before the sisters' train arrived from Preston where Isabel and Agnes had been to visit their sick mother in a sanatorium.

Jessie drove the Austin Seven the short distance from Lime Street to the office where they all disembarked complete with luggage.

Before Jessie could volunteer to make a pot of tea, George said, "I suppose it's been quiet here in our absence." Jessie was unable to suppress her mirth but managed to say, "George, I will tell you all about it one day." With that she winked at Khan. George knew that was a sign not to pursue the matter.

Isabel walked over to the filing cabinets. On opening the top drawer, she was surprised to see a new filing system in place. "Someone's been busy whilst we were away," she said.

"You could say that," Jessie said, "now, I'm sure you would all love a cuppa."

Before Jessie reached the kitchenette, the office telephone rang. Jessie heard Agnes say, "Dale Street Private

Investigations Agency, how may I help you?" A few moments later, Agnes called out, "Jessie it's for you. The Isle of Skye police."

Immediately Jessie thought, *Fiona McTavish,* as she took the phone from Agnes. "Jessie Harper here," she announced to the caller.

"Miss Harper, Sergeant McHendry from the Isle of Skye Constabulary. I understand you have had recent dealings with a Fiona McTavish. Is that correct?"

"Indeed. A colleague and I were planning to visit her soon. Why do you ask?"

"I thought you should know poor Fiona has passed away."

"Oh, my goodness. What happened, Sergeant, can you tell me?"

"The doctor says she died of fright," Sergeant McHendry said.

The End

About KJ Cornwall

KJ Cornwall is the pen name of multi-genre bestselling author Stephen Bentley, a former British detective and barrister. It is the name associated with the Jessie Harper Paranormal Cozy Mystery series.

The series is set in 1930s Liverpool, a city the author knows well.

Why KJ Cornwall? Kathleen, the author's mother, and Jack her twin brother, are honoured by the author in the choice of this pen name.

Join KJ's mailing list here.[1] Or if you prefer use the QR code below:

---

1. KJ Cornwall Mailing List

You can join an exclusive club with access to chapter by chapter serialisation of all KJ Cornwall new releases starting with *The Vanishing Lady* here at Stephen Bentley's Ko-Fi page or use the QR code below. All members also receive the eBooks free on publication date. This applies to all Stephen Bentley books and all his pen names.

Also By KJ Cornwall

See the image below and click it to see the full updated list of books by KJ Cornwall. Use the QR code
below if you prefer.

Click the image to see details and
all retailers of all of the books in
the series at Books2Read.

Books2Read

9 798230 341208